STRANGE SEED

STRANGE SEED

A Novel by

T.M. WRIGHT

Everest House
Publishers   New York

This book is for Chris.

It is equally, though for different
reasons, for Nana.

Where did you come from, baby dear?
Out of the everywhere, into here.

— Song from "At the back of the North Wind"

MAY 1957
DOWNSTATE NEW YORK

The tall man curses sharply in reaction to the sudden pain. The pain fades slowly; the man turns to his son beside him and says, "Not a word to repeat, son. Not a word to repeat."

The child looks on wonderingly. "Yes, father," he says.

The pain returns and the tall man curses again, and again. When the pain subsides, he says once more, "Not a word to repeat, son. Not a word to—" But the pain, renewing itself, chokes the sentence off.

The man slumps, groaning, to his knees.

"Father?" the child says. "Father?"

The pain subsides, but not as much as before, and the man shakes his head slowly, in confusion.

It occurs to him that he's dying, and his acceptance of it is quick, nearly casual. Because there are more important considerations: As a by-product of his death, his son will be left alone at the secluded farmhouse.

Through the pain—lingering dully at the back of his head—the man motions to his son to come over. The child obeys, and the man pulls him close. "Go to . . . Mr. Lumas," he whispers, "down . . ." And again the pain stops his words.

"Father?" the child says. "Father?"

He's more confused than I am, the man thinks, despite the pain.

He tries to speak again. But speech is beyond him.

A quivering smile shivers along his lips. He curses spontaneously, and falls face forward onto the wet earth.

The last few weeks, the rain has been nearly continuous; the earth gives testimony to it. All about, the things that come out of the earth are showing themselves. The thickets bordering the field are a vibrant green. The small pine forest to the west—all winter and spring no more than a monotone darkness—seems in motion, as if in anticipation of summer and the changes it will bring.

"Father?" the child says. "Father?"

The tall man lies still. A burying beetle—small and efficient—probes tentatively at his chin.

Around the tall man, the earth lives, the earth produces, and swells a little in expectation of what this recent death will give it (only one of many thousands of deaths that second).

"Get up, father," the child says. "Father?"

The child waits. What he has known from his father until this moment has been life. He has seen his father strain for hours at a stuck plow; he has seen him smile wearily at the end of the day; he has heard curses from him, and, each time, "Not a word to repeat, son. Not a word to repeat." And he has seen him in the act of love —the act of life.

"Father? Get up, Father." There was small magic in the words before. There is no magic now.

4

The child waits.

Night comes.

The child continues to wait.

There is more bewilderment than grief in the child now—a bewilderment with immense capabilities. For, around him, things the earth has produced are becoming bold with curiosity. One creature is within arm's reach, but—and not because of the moonless dark—the child does not sense its presence.

The creature waits. Because of all that the earth has produced in recent weeks, its belly is full, and so it is merely curious. After many minutes, it moves off.

The child continues to wait.

Other things that the earth has produced—some as large as the child, some larger, and some so small he could not see them, even in daylight—move closer and form a very rough circle around the child and the tall man. Still, the child is ignorant of their presence.

There are words prodding at the child's consciousness—words that, in concert with his slowly fading bewilderment and increasing grief, have much to do with his ignorance of what surrounds him. For he has no fear. His father's words have long since obliterated fear: "There is nothing here to harm you, son—unless you invite harm." And, "You are as much a part of this as any living thing."

The child waits. Eventually, the moonless dark lightens; a false dawn, but the end of darkness.

"Father?" he says. "Father?" The word is so mechanical now that he does not realize he's said it.

He turns, hesitates, looks back at the gray, elongated mass that is his father.

And goes back to the house.

The house is very quiet now—a maze of black and gray and harsh right angles. Habit soon overcomes the maze; the child makes his way to the house's second floor, to his bedroom, and settles onto the old bed. Tears come to him, though he can't yet consciously admit there is reason for tears. They trickle down the sides of his face. A dozen tears.

He is accustomed to the noises of the house.

Two dozen tears.

The noises of the house are like friends because the child has known the noises since before he realized the house was making them. Vaguely he knows that the earth is partly responsible. That the earth swells and recedes, swells and recedes. Not as if it were restless—only breathing. Because the earth, like himself, must breathe, and the house—a part of the earth—must breathe with it.

Three dozen tears. The pillow soaks them up.

Groaning noises; if a man were responsible, wouldn't he be very much like a scarecrow, or a stick man? Rasping, groaning noises. Wood sounds. And the distant spray-of-water sounds—the windows being pushed at by the wind.

Four dozen tears.

And the scratch and skitter sounds of the other living creatures in the walls of the house.

The tears stop.

It is a creative house. Occasionally, there are new and often fleeting noises whose source is hard to pinpoint. Only half consciously, the child listens to just such noises now. And waits, expectation growing in him.

After a long moment, he calls, "Father? Is that you?" He props himself up in the bed and continues to listen. He strains to see, but sees little.

"Father?" he repeats, though with uncertainty, because the noises his father's footfalls make on the stairs are of a different sort—more pronounced, more purpose-ful.

The noises stop.

The child sleeps.

THE MORNING

Realization, like punishment, comes swiftly to the child. And, as to punishment, he winces and stifles a moan. Here, in the bright sunlight, denial is impossible. He sees that his father's body is becoming what swamps are made of, and soil is made of—becoming food for the horsetail, and clover, and burying beetles, and a million others. Because the earth, the breathing earth, must be constantly nourished.

His father's words are closer now, and understandable. "Decay is not the grim thing it appears to be. It is renewal."

"Father?" the child pleads, realizing the futility of the word. "Father?" he repeats, more in memory of those times his father responded to the word than for any other reason.

Father?—distantly, from the thickets to the south.

Father? Barely audible.

The child looks questioningly up from his father's body. "Father?" he calls.

Father?

An echo, the child thinks. Months before, he remembers, in the heart of the forest, "Hello," extended, "Hello," repeated, "Hello," shouted back at both of them, father and son, by the voices of the forest.

"Hello," the child calls.

Father? replies the voice of the thickets.

"Hello," the child calls. And distantly, from the east,

7

from the forest, "Hello, Hello, Hello," decreasing in intensity. And finally, nothing.

Hello—from the thickets.

"Hello," the child calls.

Hello.

"Hello, Father!" the child calls.

And the forest replies, "Hello, Father! Hello, Father!"

And the voice of the thickets replies, *Hello, Father! Father? Hello!*

THE PRESENT

CHAPTER 1

Rachel Griffin listened to an unfamiliar crowd of sounds—the varied chortlings of toads and frogs, the moanings and screechings of owls, the whir and squeak and twitter of a million insects. Occasionally, the wind moving over shards of glass in the window frames at the back of the small room added—to the sounds of the rural night—a dissonant set of high-pitched whining noises, like a family of small tin birds calling at a distance.

Rachel felt, in the crowd of sounds, the conspicuous absence of the sounds of man. She wished for the groan of traffic, for the comforting, hollow noises of radios and TVs, even for the neighbors having one of their periodic arguments. But those, she knew, were the sounds of places that were far beyond her, places that—despite their many shortcomings—had variously served as home for nearly all her twenty-six years and therefore didn't give her the dismal sense of aloneness that this place gave her.

"Paul?" she said.

Paul Griffin turned from the window and saw that his wife was sitting up on the old overstuffed couch; he sensed that she was watching him intently, wonderingly.

"Did I wake you?" he asked.

"No. I haven't been able to sleep." She hesitated. "Is something wrong, Paul?"

"Nothing's wrong." A pause. "It's that floor. Have you ever tried to sleep on the floor? It's impossible." He felt himself grimace; lies, even half-truths—as the remark had been—had never come easily to him. He was thankful for the near-total darkness, thankful it hid him. Rachel would know his deception, otherwise.

"Do you want to use the couch, Paul?"

"No." He made a nebulous gesture with his arm. "Go back to sleep, Rachel. I'll be to bed soon."

She wrapped herself in the large blue quilt she and Paul had been sharing and, stumbling once on the quilt's trailing edges, joined him at the window. He put his arm around her. "You really should be asleep," he told her.

"Uh-huh."

He could dimly see her face now. In the classic sense, he knew, it was not a particularly beautiful face. The full, dark eyebrows were complemented by the large, oval brown eyes and high forehead. Her mouth appeared to be in a constant pout because of a slight, natural downturn at its outside edges and was as full and nearly as dark as her brows—that fullness was offset by a strong jawline and a long, gently muscled neck. It was a face, Paul mused, whose individual parts had struggled for preeminence; at last, a pleasing balance had been established.

He kissed her. "Thank you," he said.

"For what?"

"For not being able to sleep without me."

She smiled. "Our first night in our first house, Paul." It had seemed, she realized, an accusation.

"Yes," Paul said. He wanted to add, *Our first and, I hope, our last house*, but knew she'd sense the dishonesty in the remark. "The first of many nights, Rachel."

She leaned against him and mumbled what he thought to be an affirmative.

I'm uncomfortable with this house, Paul. It frightens me. I've never lived here before; you have. And that gives you an advantage.

"We've got our work cut out for us, Rachel."

"Yes. Yes, we do."

What do I know about houses like this, Paul? About this kind of life? It's too quiet here. There's too little light. We get used to noise and light. We grow to identify with it, no matter how much we deny it.

"I can't imagine why anyone would want to smash the windows like this, Rachel." He fingered a fragment of glass protruding from the window frame. "I can't imagine," he continued, "why they'd want to do any of the shitty things they did."

Rachel nodded slightly. *Why indeed, Paul?* She had assumed that "country people" bore an almost instinctive respect for the rights and property of others. But the house's condition had caused her to rethink that assumption: people, she'd decided, were the same everywhere; country people, city people—it made no difference.

"But it's basically a very sound house," Paul went on. He pushed against the window casing with the palm of his hand. "At least there's nothing structurally wrong with it."

Rachel nodded again. "Let's go back to bed, Paul. It's late."

"You go ahead, darling. I'll join you in a minute." He put his hands on her shoulders and gently turned

13

her around to face the couch. "Go ahead," he repeated.

Reluctantly, she went back to the couch, lay down, and adjusted the quilt so a good portion of it fell to the floor, where Paul, for lack of a better place, had chosen to sleep. "Don't be too long, Paul."

"Just a minute or two."

Rachel closed her eyes. *Yes,* she thought, *Paul had the advantage. The house charmed him. He had come home. The transition would be easy for him, if it hadn't already occurred. He was comfortable here. With the ghosts of his mother and his father and his boyhood self . . .*

"Are you asleep, Rachel?" Softly.

"No."

"Oh . . . I was going to go outside for a minute."

"I wish you wouldn't, Paul."

"You could come with me if you'd like."

"It's too cold . . . no." She paused. "It *is* late, Paul."

"I'll just be a minute."

"I wish . . ." But he had already crossed through the large kitchen and was heading for the back door.

"Try to get to sleep," he called. In the next moment he closed the door behind him.

Henry Lumas' night vision was excellent. What would have appeared to other, less sensitive eyes as only a vaguely elongated, nearly amorphous mass, Lumas knew to be the tall, thin young man who'd just moved into what had been the Schmidt House.

Paul? Yes, that was the young man's name. And his wife's name was Rachel. A good name.

They were city people—that was obvious to anyone with eyes and ears. How stiffly the young man walked, as if in pain; he was accustomed to the kind of awful confinement that only cities impose on a man.

14

She—his wife—moved gracefully enough, but as if it was expected of her, as if she granted her favors reluctantly, out of a sense of duty. And that was unfortunate.

Curses, as well, came too easily to the young man. He lacked patience (although, Lumas reflected, finding the house in that condition, the man had had good reason to curse). He was quick-tempered. He probably expected perfection, or at least that things run far more smoothly than things possibly could. If so, life here would be a revelation. Nothing ran smoothly here. You depended on nothing, you counted on nothing. Only the bad.

The Schmidts had learned that quick enough. When, in the space of six months, their two children had died—one of pneumonia, the other of a disease even the doctor from town couldn't diagnose—they'd learned.

These people would learn too. They'd have to learn.

Across the darkened, weed-choked fields that separated him from the house, Lumas saw that Paul was looking his way.

"Hello," Paul shouted. "Hello."

For a moment, Lumas thought of answering. Then he saw that Paul had turned and was going back into the house.

Lumas hesitated a second. It was unlikely that the young man had seen him, though of no significance if he had. He—Lumas—would introduce himself soon enough and offer the young couple his skills as a carpenter.

He turned. What demanded his attention now were the traps he'd set out at various points in the forest. Maybe one of the traps would hold more than the fly-ridden stump of some luckless animal's hind leg.

For too long, that was all the traps had yielded.

"Paul?" Rachel called. "Is that you?" She sat up and peered into the kitchen.

"Yes, it's me. Were you expecting someone else?"

"No, I was . . ." She paused. "Who were you calling to out there, Paul?"

"No one." He crossed the room and sat next to her on the couch. "I just wanted to hear my echo. That's pretty silly, huh."

She smiled weakly. "It's late, Paul. You said that man —Mr. Marsh?—you said he was going to pick you up at seven."

"Yes," Paul said. "I know." Rachel wondered if the trace of annoyance evident in his tone was because she'd reminded him, or because there were only a few hours of sleep remaining. She tried—not very successfully, because of the darkness—to study his angular face, the deep-set, hazel eyes. "Tell me what's wrong, Paul."

He raised his eyebrows briefly—a gesture Rachel had learned was indicative of confusion. "It's all very . . . discouraging, isn't it?" he said. "Maybe it was a bad idea to come here. This house and . . . and the condition it's in—it must all be quite a shock to you." He took her hand. "I mean," he went on, his tone oddly paternalistic, "this isn't New York City, is it?"

"No," was all Rachel could manage to say; Paul's sudden mood had taken her by surprise.

"I've told you . . . you know what it's like here, Rachel. But that really doesn't mean very much—it means nothing —until you've experienced it."

"Paul, I—"

"No, no. Let me finish." He inhaled deeply. "I think maybe I'm asking too much of you; that the . . . burdens of life here"—he grinned self-consciously—"may be, I don't know—too much for you. It takes one hell of a readjustment, more than not being able to run to the grocery store or to a movie—so much more . . ." He paused; Rachel realized what he wanted from her. She squeezed his hand reassuringly.

"Paul, I'm *not* a weak woman. I'll be able to make the adjustment."

"I didn't say you were weak, only . . . accustomed to . . . well, what I mean is—New York and this place . . ."

"Paul, you'll just have to take my word for it. If you can make the adjustment, then so can I."

Five minutes later—sooner than she'd hoped—she had convinced him.

CHAPTER 2

Rachel struck the match; it flared briefly and went out. Damn it!" she murmured.

She straightened. There were just a few matches left, and it was unlikely, even if one stayed lit, that she'd be able to get a fire started; she had never used a wood-burner, had seen them only as museum pieces. And besides, the firewood piled next to the huge, black iron stove—firewood left there by the Schmidts—was probably too damp. Why, for God's sake, hadn't Paul cut some fresh wood before going into town early that morning with Marsh? He could have shown her how to use the stove—if *he* knew.

No fire meant no hot water, and that meant she wouldn't be able to scrub the kitchen walls. The vandals had spattered the normally yellow walls with fireplace ash, mud, and what had proved to be a mixture of urine and feces. Cleaning the walls would go a long way toward relieving her of the pessimism that gripped her.

It must, she mused, have been a parting act of vandalism. The walls in the other rooms, except for the living room's south wall—the other side was the kitchen's north wall—remained virtually untouched. Yes. The artist signing his work. She caught herself on the thought: Paul had been right when he'd referred to "the bastards," more than one. And he'd been right when he'd pointed out that the vandals had doubtlessly come to the house from one of the "neighboring" farms, or from town, expressly for the purpose of vandalism; the narrow, unpaved road in front of the house ended a quarter mile north, and there were no other houses on it along its three-mile span. Quite obviously, the house had not been the random target of some transient pack of vandals—the vandalism had been purposeful.

Wincing, Rachel remembered the string of vicious obscenities that had erupted from Paul when he'd first seen the house. John Marsh, who'd driven them the ten miles from Penn Yan—because their own wretched eight-year-old Ford wagon had failed there; was now awaiting a new carburetor; "Coupla days, Mr. Griffin—it's gotta be ordered," the mechanic said—had merely looked dumbfounded. "I dunno," he mumbled. "I dunno."

"You were supposed to keep an eye on the goddamned place!" Paul shouted at him.

Marsh continued to look dumbfounded. He said nothing.

"My uncle and I *paid* you to keep an eye on it!"

"I dunno," Marsh repeated. "I dunno."

"That," Paul hissed, "is obvious!"

"I come up every week, Mr. Griffin. Sometimes two times a week. And I never seen nobody around."

"Well, it's clear you didn't use . . ."

"Paul, please," Rachel had cut in. She looked at Marsh. "I apologize for my husband. He's understandably upset—"

"I'll do my own apologizing," Paul interrupted, "if it's necessary. And I don't think it is." He got out of the car

19

and faced the house with his hands on his hips. "Jesus Christ!" he muttered. "Jesus goddamned Christ!" He glanced around at Rachel and Marsh. "Well, c'mon," he said. "We might as well see what the bastards have done."

Certain aspects of the vandalism, Rachel reflected now, had mystified her and Paul and Marsh. Although smashing each of the house's dozen windows had been a rather pedestrian thing to do—windows were made to be smashed —defecating on every article of furniture, except for the red overstuffed couch in the living room, had been a bit less pedestrian, though it took little imagination, and tearing each of the house's four inner doors off its hinges, then smashing each beyond any hope of repair, indicated some larger purpose, a purpose beyond mere senseless vandalism.

In the decrepit, apparently never used second-floor front bedroom they had found the remains of the animal.

"Looks like a coon," Marsh observed. "Got caught in a trap would be my guess from the condition of its hind leg there." He pointed stiffly. "It must've chewed itself loose. Some animals do that, you know—they chew right through the bones and all."

Rachel had grimaced severely at the remark. Coupled with the condition of the house and the gloomy prospects for its livability once the damage had been repaired, the remark had forcefully understruck a fact Rachel had, up to that point, been reluctant to admit: Here, at the house, she was very much out of her depth. What she had known— up until her marriage to Paul six months before—had been a small, stiflingly warm apartment on Seventy-fifth Street near Broadway, a wearisome sales job at the West Town House—dealers in expensive and essentially useless wicker and rattan furniture—a tall, hairy-chested, unfriendly man named Rinaldo who weekly took nearly one third of her paycheck for not quite a week's worth of groceries, and several very polite, very gay young men who seemed to take turns walking her home if—as often occurred—she had to work late. (That confusing routine seemed to emerge shortly after she had begun working at the West Town House two years before, a month or so after she had come to New York from Rochester, near Lake Ontario. It had been a move designed to put a lot of painful memories behind her, if only physically: So many amateur philosophers and psychologists said that that sort of thing never worked, but it had. At least in her case. Or perhaps it had only been a matter of time.)

She met Paul a year after her arrival in New York, when the city was on the verge of becoming either "her city" or "that hateful city." And she had almost decided "her city" because it was, after all, only a very big city filled mostly with very small people, like herself.

"Hi." Paul, on Seventy-first Street, in front of The Red Apple, Rinaldo's grocery. It was an uncomfortably warm evening in April. "You've dropped a can of something there."

She turned, smiled warily, politely.

He pointed to just behind her. "Here, let me get it," he said. "Your hands are pretty full, aren't they?"

"Yes," she managed. "Thank you."

And it had started.

Several nights later, Paul had invited himself to her apartment.

He managed a small department store, he said; "Griffin's," owned by his Uncle Harry. He had managed it a long time, too long—had lived in New York most of his life, ever since his father died. What did she do? he wondered. How long had she been in New York (he seemed to sense she was not a native)? What were her long-range plans? So little about himself. A born salesman, she had thought at the time. Make the other person talk. Be the listener. Everyone wants to talk about themselves. How transparent. Just another stud on the make—he was only a little more charming, a little more introspective, a little more intelligent (and so, more dangerous) than the others.

But, happily, though he *was* more charming, intelligent, introspective, he hadn't been trying to use those virtues to his advantage. He had been genuinely interested. Genuinely liked her. Genuinely wanted to get to know her better.

He succeeded.

And a half year after their first meeting they were married.

A month after their marriage, Paul made his announcement:

"Ever been downstate, Rachel? In the Naples, Penn Yan area, I mean. It's nice country. A bit poverty-stricken, maybe, but nice."

"I've driven through it."

"Did you like it?"

"It was okay, I suppose. Why?"

"We're going to live there."

Silence.

"I've been planning it for quite a while, Rachel. I've got it all worked out. The house, everything."

"But . . . I thought, uh . . . I thought New York . . ."

"Was my city?"

"I suppose . . ."

"Yes, it is. You might call me a hard-core New Yorker, as a matter of fact." He paused briefly, frowned a little. "And because of that—how do I put it?—because of that hard-core New Yorker in me, I feel, uh, unclean. Jaded. Do you understand?"

"I don't know." Hesitantly, confusedly. "I guess so."

"I wasn't born here."

"Yes, I know."

"I was born at my father's house. Our house now.

22

Have I ever told you about that house?"

"You've mentioned it. You said it was 'primitive.' That's the word you used—'primitive.' "

"A good word, under the circumstances. It's a turn-of-the-century kind of farmhouse. Low ceilings, small windows, no . . . amenities, though the last tenants—the Schmidts, that was their name—did install a gasoline-powered electric generator." He grinned.

"Sounds terrific, Paul."

"Don't be sarcastic, please."

"I just wish you had mentioned these . . . plans before."

"I'm mentioning them now. And I have hinted at them, haven't I?"

"If you did, you were very subtle about it, Paul." She paused briefly. "You're *telling* me now. And I don't know if I like that. I'd *like* to have been consulted."

"You don't want to do it?"

"I didn't say that. You've got to give me some time to think about it. And you've got to give me reasons."

"Well, I've already given you reasons. They may seem kind of flimsy . . ." Rachel smiled. "But they go deeper," he continued. "Much deeper. Call them emotional ties, if you want."

"You can't go home again, Paul."

"Oh, c'mon. You can too." His tone severe, impatient, as if Rachel's remark had been impossibly inane.

She said nothing, appeared hurt.

"I'm sorry. I didn't mean to snap at you. But I really do have this whole thing worked out. I've put a chunk of my paycheck away each week for the last six years, ever since I took over ownership of the house from my uncle—all in anticipation of this night."

"You anticipated *me*, Paul?"

"Yes." Flatly, as if it was not quite as distasteful a fact

23

as it appeared on the surface. "Or someone like you." She raised her eyebrows at that. "It turned out to be you," he went on inanely, "which pleases me." He paused. "It pleases me a lot."

Thankfully, she seemed to understand. After a moment's silence, she said, "And what about when your savings run out? What do we do then?"

"Oh, that's the best part." His face lit up with enthusiasm. "We're going to live off the land, Rachel." He paused briefly. "Isn't that a nice phrase," he continued, " 'live off the land.' I like that phrase."

"And I repeat," Rachel said, "how terrific."

"Yes, it is," he conceded, his enthusiasm still strong despite the remark. "But that doesn't make it impossible, does it? No. It doesn't. Just . . . difficult."

"You are *not* a farmer, Paul. You're kidding yourself."

"You may be right. I've taken some agriculture courses and such. I have a working technical knowledge of the whole thing, I think. Though it won't really be commercial farming, of course. Just enough for us to live on, maybe a little more. And maybe I can get a part-time job in town, I don't know. But you may be right. Maybe, at heart, I'm a New Yorker and nothing more. But, dammit, I'm going to find out for myself. It's a move I've wanted to make for a long, long time, Rachel."

After a week of what Paul called discussion, and Rachel called argument, plans for the move from New York City to Upstate were under way.

Rachel set the box of matches on top of the stove, went over and peered out the kitchen's small back window.

Well, she thought after her eyes had adjusted to the sunlight, it was all rather pleasant, wasn't it? Something like Central Park, though, of course, a great deal larger.

Larger, and far more colorful, and obviously wilder. Much wilder.

She reconsidered. There was, she sensed, a kind of order, a kind of symmetry here. It was difficult to pinpoint, almost subliminal, but present nonetheless. A curious thing.

She frowned. *Take me back*, she thought. *Paul, come home and take me back to what I know.* She realized—though she would not have admitted it—that the words formed a very gentle, unimpassioned plea. That she was vulnerable.

This place, the land around the farmhouse, was moist with life. Life had been allowed to run rampant, unchecked, and it had sought its own level. There was a certain frantic harmony to it, understandably discomforting, she reasoned, to a person like herself whose only previous acquaintance with harmony had been at Carnegie Hall, at the Metropolitan Opera, and in poetry. But those were imitations. The harmony of fields and forest and color had been their model. But, understanding this—albeit in a vague, oblique way—didn't make it any less discomforting. The frantic harmony she sensed here—had sensed, she knew, from her first moment at the house—was at odds with what she'd grown accustomed to.

She fingered the top buttons of her blouse. Yes—she smiled—they were fastened.

She froze. Those were footfalls, she realized, on the steep and dry-rotted back steps.

Henry Lumas hoped that Rachel would react differently than the Schmidt woman had. "No, no," the woman had repeated over and over again—either out of anguish or an unlikely embarrassment, Lumas had not been sure—and clutching stupidly at her bosom all the while, as if protecting it or denying it. A minute later, Lumas had found himself standing before a closed and locked door.

Well, he considered, he came bearing the gift of firewood this time, and an offer of his services as a carpenter. How could the young woman refuse him?

He studied the house. From this distance, there was little evidence of the violence it had sustained. It was a small house, some would have called it quaint. The aged green-shingled walls and gray-stone roof blended nicely with the surrounding land. Indeed, Lumas remembered, near sunset on certain nights—especially when the house was empty, as it had been for two years—it became invisible, as if the earth had taken it back into herself. It was only when you drew very close to it, day or night, that the illusion of oneness with the earth faded. People had built it and lived in it. The rough, yard-wide area between the bottom of the crude back steps and the two wooden poles twenty feet away was a place where nothing grew, not even the heartiest weeds—several generations of women had hung their just-washed clothes between those poles. And there were narrow spaces along the cobblestone cellar wall where cementing material seemed not quite as weathered as it should; these were once empty spaces, the homes of wasps, homes that had been destroyed by one of the house's many tenants. At the front of the house, some young romantic had carved the initials "J.S." and, below it, the name "Mary" in the trunk of the huge century-old elm that had recently lost one of its primary limbs to a vicious electrical storm. Someone—the Schmidts, Lumas supposed—had applied a coat of light brown paint to the frame of the kitchen window, probably the start of an abortive attempt to repaint and reshingle the entire house.

Lumas was roused from his momentary reverie by movement at the window. He looked closely; there was a face at the window. Had the husband returned so soon? No, he saw, it was the woman—Rachel. There—the gentle

26

slope of her shoulders, the dark oval face, the darker hair falling to her breasts. As still as she was, she looked like a permanent fixture in the window. Lumas shuddered a little at the thought: Near the end, the Schmidt woman had presented much the same picture at the larger, second-floor window. At first, he'd thought the woman had been offering herself to him but, drawing closer to the house, had seen that her gaze had not been on him, that her nakedness had been—it was hard to imagine—somehow for her own benefit, not his. After many minutes, Lumas remembered, she'd become aware of his presence and, with an oddly low-pitched shriek, had violently pulled the shade closed.

Lumas hefted the awkward load of firewood he carried in his arms. Better to walk the weed-choked and heavily rutted path a hundred feet to his left, he thought, than these fields. A heavy rain three nights before had made walking them precarious.

CHAPTER 3

The buck had lived off the vegetation in the forests and fields for eight years. He was one of the hunted, but man had done away with his hunters—the mountain lion and the wolf—or had driven them farther north, into Canada. So the life of the buck, in comparison with many of the other wild creatures, had been peaceful. His knowledge of death, and the necessity of it, was negligible. He'd seen men, but only from a distance, and he'd wondered, in a vague, instinctively cautious way, what sort of creatures they were. But men had never lain eyes on him.

The buck nibbled contentedly at the chokecherry bush. As he nibbled, he half-listened to the small sounds around him; there, the sound of a raccoon shuffling through the grass to wash itself at the stream a few yards away; there, the tapping of a woodpecker against a large sycamore near the edges of the forest; from far above, the endless screechings of a hawk; all around, the drone of a million insects. The sounds coalesced. They were morning sounds, and the buck was familiar with them. There was no danger in the sounds.

The buck stopped nibbling. He listened, his body tensed and ready for flight, to the new sounds—the sounds of something heavy and not quite as graceful as himself moving toward him from behind, from the area of the stream. Above the sounds was the hawk, and nothing else. All the other creatures had quieted. The leaves of the chokecherry bush rustled a little in a tentative wind, masking the slight sounds of the thing behind.

CHAPTER 4

Paul looked askance at the new bed. "It won't do, will it?" he said. "It's too big." He had chosen a huge, dark oak four-poster; it dominated fully one third of the small square room. "I'll take it back, Rachel. I'll get another one."

Rachel sat on the bed and pushed on its mattress with the palms of her hands. "Don't be silly," she said. "It's perfect. I love it."

"No," Paul said. "You think it's cumbersome."

"I think we'll be able to sleep on it. That's what I think."

"Uh-huh. And get lost on it, too. I don't know what possessed me to buy the damned thing." He shrugged his shoulders, abandoning the subject. "I talked to that man about the windows," he went on. "He said something about a month's wait for the window glass, that I should have taken measurements. I told him that was his job, wasn't it? And he said it was, but that it would require two trips out here instead of one, that the extra trip would cost me twenty dollars, and if I wanted to save that twenty dollars I should take the measurements myself and telephone him. I told him we didn't have a phone and he said something about 'foolish back-to-the-landers,' something like that. Then he asked where I was from, I told him New York and he started chuckling. Anyway, he ended up saying we wouldn't last six months before we started itching to get back to the city."

"You should have told him you were born here, Paul."

"Why? I don't care what he thinks. He's nobody. And he's wrong." He paused as if trying to forget the man. "By the way, about a phone: That's going to take a while, too. Seems they have to string wire and that takes time. And money."

"We're going to have one, aren't we?"

"Eventually, yes. In a couple months. It won't be so bad without one. We'll survive."

"I suppose. If it can't be helped . . ." She sighed heavily. "Did you check to see if the car was ready?"

"Uh-huh. It isn't. Shit, I'm tempted to go out and get another one. I *would* if I thought the economics would work out, if a used car would be worth what I've got to put into the Ford to keep it running. But I think it's just the carburetor, and that's only going to be fifty dollars or so. I doubt I could get a decent used car for that much."

"You're probably right," Rachel said, obviously unconvinced. "So what are you going to do, hire Marsh as your chauffeur until the car's ready?"

"No." He grinned. "We've got all the food and gasoline we need"—gasoline for the generator—"for the time being. No, the mechanic said a week. I won't need Marsh till then. I asked him to come back anyway on Friday, just in case."

Rachel sighed again. "And what about the windows, Paul?"

He waved agitatedly at the bedroom window. "We'll

cover them, I guess. There's scrap wood in the barn. It'll look like hell, I know—"

"It'll be dark as a cave," Rachel protested.

"Well, it can't be helped, I'm sorry."

A moment's silence followed, then Paul made a complex gesture designed to indicate the rest of the house. "I like what you did here today. It makes the house more presentable."

"Oh yes, that." She paused meaningfully. "I forgot to tell you; we had a visitor. A man named Lumas."

"Lumas?"

"Henry Lumas. He said he knew you."

"I don't know anyone named Lumas. Did you let him into the house?"

"He said he *knew* you, Paul. I told him our name was Griffin, and he said, 'Griffin? Your husband's father's name wasn't Sam, was it?' I said yes, and he said he'd known your father, and that he knew you."

Paul sat next to her on the bed and shook his head slowly, condemningly.

"He said he *knew* you," Rachel repeated. "And besides, he's just a harmless old man. He brought us some firewood. That's how I was able to get a fire started. He showed me how it's done."

"I really wish," Paul began, "that you wouldn't let strangers into the house when I'm not here. New York City should have taught you that much. How do you know this man wasn't responsible for . . ." He made a long, slow sweeping motion with his arm. "For all this? How do you know?"

"I don't, Paul. But I think I'm a good enough judge of character to—"

"Just promise that you'll never again let someone into the house when I'm not here."

She sighed. "I promise."

32

"Good." He paused. "Did this man stay long?" His tone was vaguely apologetic.

"No," Rachel answered after a moment. "No, he just brought the firewood in, we talked awhile, and he left. He's really quite a harmless old man, Paul. He's got this great mound of white hair—he looks like an emaciated Moses. Well, he's not really emaciated, just very thin. Wiry. He lives in a little cabin out in the woods." She nodded at the west wall of the room. "He says he's been living there for close to twenty years. He knew your father very well, apparently."

"Oh?" Grudging interest.

"Yes. He had nothing but good to say about him. He said it was a real shame he died so young."

"He was," Paul told her, "only thirty-six."

"*That* young, Paul? I didn't know."

Paul smiled feebly and cupped his hands in front of his knees. "Someday," he said, "I'll tell you about my last week or so here, after my father died, I mean. It makes . . . interesting after-dinner talk."

"Yes, I'd like that, Paul." She looked questioningly at him. "I'm sorry," she continued. "That sounded callous, didn't it? You've always been so secretive about that part of your life. It must be . . ." She searched for the right word. "It must be painful to talk about it."

"No," he answered. "Not painful." *Confusing*, he wanted to say, but it would require an explanation, and he wasn't up to that. "Just unpleasant, I suppose." A smile that Rachel mistook for self-pity flashed across his mouth. "I'll tell you about it sometime." He stood abruptly. "Now we've got work to do. Maybe I can put up some of those shingles on the east wall of the house before nightfall."

"Do you think the vandals were responsible for that, too—for ripping those shingles down?"

"Probably." He reached into his pocket, withdrew a

measuring tape. "Here," he began; he handed the tape to Rachel. "You can measure some of these doorways while I'm outside. Marsh has some doors that might fit."

Rachel took the tape from him and studied it briefly. "I just take the inside measurements, right?"

He smiled. "That's right. It shouldn't be too difficult for a bright girl like you."

She returned his smile. "Don't be so sure, Paul. I *am* female, you remember—very weak, very dependent, et cetera, et cetera." She made little, coy, mincing motions with her mouth and hands.

Paul's smile broadened.

"I mean," she went on, "anything other than breakfast-making, baby-making, and love-making . . . well, I'm just a babbling idiot."

Paul laughed suddenly—a genuine laugh. It was the first time he'd laughed since they'd come to the house and it told Rachel that the tension she'd sensed in him was decreasing.

"You don't agree, Paul?" Rachel asked. She held the measuring tape extended between her outstretched arms. "See all the numbers on this thing, Paul? It's *very* confusing."

His laughter increased.

That's nice, Paul, she wanted to say, but knew it would make him self-conscious. *That's more like your old self.*

His laughter subsided. "Thank you," he said.

"For what?"

He leaned over and kissed her on the forehead. "Just . . . thank you."

He left the room.

It was all much better now, Rachel told herself. She leaned against the living room doorway and folded her arms across her stomach. And it hadn't taken much to make it better. Just a few odds and ends of furniture—a white wicker chair, hers; a red winged-back chair, Paul's; a small cherry-wood table, a rolltop writing desk, very old, a brightly colored rug, and, most importantly, plans to erase the awful damage done to the house. That wasn't much. In time it would be quite a beautiful little house. One day, she might even be able to call it home.

She felt something tickling her ankle. She looked: "Hello, cat," she said. She'd have to think of a name for the animal, of course. She couldn't go on calling it "cat," although Paul seemed to feel it was all that was required. "It's not like it's a bona fide member of the family," he'd told her. "It's just a cat, and it's supposed to be quite a mouser. God knows this house needs one."

She stroked the cat, pleased by the upward-thrusting motions of its huge gray head. "I don't care what Paul says," she cooed. "You're going to have a name, like everyone else."

Laughter! It had been a long time since Henry Lumas had heard laughter from within that house. The Schmidts had been too gloomy and self-involved for it, which might have been part of their undoing. They had dwelled too much on what vexed them, hadn't laughed enough, or joked enough, or just felt good often enough.

Sam Griffin had known how to feel good and how to laugh. He'd had his share of trouble, more trouble than ordinary men, but, up to the day the earth took him, he had been happy with himself. And that counted as much as enough sun, or enough rain, or easy winters, or bright strong children. It counted *more*, as a matter of fact.

Lumas watched as Paul clumsily hammered a shingle into place, stepped back, and gauged the accuracy of his work. "Damn," Paul murmured; the shingle was slightly out of line. He ripped one of the nails out, repositioned the shingle, put another nail into it, and stepped back again.

"That's better," he said aloud.

"You want some help there, young man?" Lumas called.

CHAPTER 5

The rabbit knew nothing about death. It had lived forever, it would continue to live forever. Still, there were the predators. The fox, the great horned owl, the red-tailed hawk. And the others.

Instinct did not tell the rabbit that its enemies required its death, only that its flesh would make a satisfying meal. So when the rabbit's lungs refused to work because its throat had been crushed, it slid into death not as frantically as its killer might; no memories or sympathies crowded back. Its eyes opened wide, its always twitching nose stopped twitching, its muscles tensed, as if readying themselves for use, and it died.

Then its body was carried away by the ears for use as food. And its killer was neither joyful nor saddened because of the killing. Its killer had been beset by hunger and a craving for meat. And the rabbit had not been as cautious as it could have been.

CHAPTER 6

Rachel pushed her chair away from the desk and glanced at the dozen crumpled sheets in the wastebasket to her left, all abortive attempts at a letter to her mother.

"Damn," she whispered.

Each sheet bore at least a few paragraphs, but they were inadequate—either too subtle (her mother would think she was hiding something) or too full of small talk (which her mother disliked) or too enmeshed in weighty philosophizing about her "new life" (her mother would believe she was being pretentious, or, which was worse, idealistic).

But this last one came close, didn't it? She picked it up from the desk.

Dear Mom,

I'm sorry about that depressing phone call. Expect better from this. The house has changed, so my mood has changed. Not that I'm "comfortable" here yet, but I'm getting there.

The work we've done has helped. The mess we

found the house in three weeks ago shocked us both
—it was like a slap in the face, especially for Paul
and all the plans he'd made. We actually thought
about going back; even now I don't know why we
didn't. Laziness, maybe.

I can't say I'm hopeful, but at least I'm not
as darkly pessimistic as I was. My mistake, I believe, was in looking for parallels between life here
and life in the city. There are no parallels; New
York and this place are two different worlds. I'm
learning to appreciate that, and to accept it. Not that
I've totally succeeded. Some mornings I wake up
expecting to hear the sounds of a city awakening
around me but, instead, there's silence (though if
you only listen hard you realize it's not silence at
all). At such times, I find that I've momentarily lost
track of where I am.

There are other things. For instance, yesterday
Paul and Mr. Lumas (did I mention him in my last
letter?) found the remains of a deer, a "six-point
buck," according to Mr. Lumas. He says that maybe
there's a wolf in the area, although Paul says that the
last wolf around here was killed decades and decades
ago. He does admit that no other animal, except a
mountain lion (and there are supposed to be none of
those here, either), could have done what was done
to this animal (all its internal organs were ripped
out—lungs, liver, etc. Pretty disgusting, the way Paul
describes it). Let me correct that: A *man* could have
done it, Lumas says. A man could have shot the animal and left it to rot. But both he and Paul examined the animal and came to the conclusion that
it had to have been attacked by a wolf, or maybe by
a very large dog, which to me seems much more
likely, though I haven't seen any dogs around.

39

At any rate, Paul bought a rifle. I've told him how much I hate those things, but he's got his mind made up and there's no way *I'm* going to change it. He's in the forest with the gun now. He took a hatchet, too—to cut firewood, he says, but since the idea of a wolf has got him very excited, I think he's gone into the woods after it rather than to cut firewood, which we have enough of anyway.

Yes, it came close. It was good enough. Damn, if only the phone were in . . .

She looked up, toward the kitchen, certain there had been a knock at the back door.

She set the unfinished letter down, listened, heard nothing.

"Who is it?" she called.

"Lumas, Mrs. Griffin," came the barely audible reply. "Henry Lumas."

The narrow path that skirted the northern edge of the fields—from the road in front of the house to the forest—ended at a swiftly moving stream. A few yards west of the stream, the land angled slightly upward; the irregular perimeter of the forest was several yards beyond.

Paul stepped gingerly across the stream and hesitated. The land here, on the slope before the forest, was not as heavily clotted with weeds as were his fields—just scatterings of horsetail, like tiny, freakish pine trees, and patches of stunted quack grass. About fifty feet to the south, close to the forest's perimeter, were two flowering dogwoods—they seemed strangely out of place, Paul thought—and just beyond, lying at a right angle to him down the slope, the mottled gray trunk of a long-dead conifer, stripped bare of branches by insects and time.

It was the darkness that struck Paul most forcibly as he looked north and south, studying the forest's perimeter. The sun's light reached only a few yards into the forest and seemed to assume a distinctly paler color, as if some curious entry fee had been taken from it.

Paul moved up the slope, cautious of how he carried the ax and the rifle—both strange burdens. He stopped. To his left, the full and overhanging branches of two beech-trees side by side formed a perfect natural archway. He studied the trees a moment, aware that they beckoned to him in a nostalgic and oddly comforting way. Then he saw two figures moving up the slope and he remembered. They were his father and himself, two decades before.

The image vanished. Paul smiled. Gripping the ax tightly, he passed beneath the archway and into the forest.

All around, small, white, three-petaled flowers—trillium—had pushed through the brownish covering of leaves and pine needles. But they were as inadequate a relief to the abrupt, nearly palpable aura of melancholy as the random and anemic shafts of daylight that slanted to earth through open spaces left by slaughtered trees.

There was, Paul thought grimly, ample evidence of man here. Although the forest was centuries upon centuries old, and many of its trees had long since succumbed to disease and weather and insects, man had picked his way through and selected only its finest and strongest specimens. Man hadn't decimated the forest, his selective cutting had merely thinned it, but the results—the insect-hollowed stumps, the anemic shafts of daylight—spoke harshly of mortality.

Here and there new growth had started; sapling hemlock—it could proliferate in the cool darkness—spruce, smatterings of ivy, climbing dodder, shelf fungus. It wasn't enough. Twenty years before, the forest had seemed so vast, and incorruptible, and eternal. Now it was involved in the incredibly slow, but inexorable, process of decay.

Trying to shake the mood that had settled over him, Paul glanced around at the beech-trees. He saw that he'd made an irregular path for himself by shuffling through the damp covering of leaves and pine needles. He'd already crossed other paths—the paths of grouse and squirrels and deer—but they were narrower, more sporadic. There was no chance, he told himself, that he'd become confused upon his return.

He remembered, suddenly, that there was a clearing of sorts—several acres of smaller, more easily managed trees. The idea of felling and stripping one of the towering, wide-girthed white pines did not appeal to him, for several reasons. Most importantly—Lumas had told him, and Lumas knew what he was talking about, didn't he?—although the forest housed several hundred of the trees, it was also one of the few remaining accessible stands in the country. A butternut tree or a birch or an oak—Lumas had also told him—would serve his needs handsomely. Or at least, he amended, the needs he had told Rachel must be met: "We can't have enough firewood, darling," he'd told her. It had been a transparent deception, he knew.

"Hello," he called suddenly. The word echoed and reechoed for a few seconds and the forest's discomforting, portentous silence returned.

He realized, suddenly, his apprehension, realized that ever since he and Lumas had found the ravaged buck he'd been apprehensive, that his casual manner with Rachel had merely been a show of bravado, an act. What did he know about wolves and how to hunt them? he asked himself. Nothing. How could he be expected to? And if he knew nothing, then what was he doing here? It was a question for which he had no answer.

Lumas, Rachel had decided weeks before, was one of those easy-to-be-with people who, unselfconsciously, allowed no lapses in the conversation; his face—regardless of what else could be said about it—was wonderfully animated, as expressive as his words. Indeed, she had often found herself more intrigued by him—the man, the character—than by his words. She very much hoped he hadn't noticed.

She glanced furtively at her watch: four o'clock—Paul would be home within an hour and would expect dinner to be ready. She'd have to excuse herself soon. Building a fire in the woodburning stove was no easy chore. Hopefully, they'd be able to replace the stove with something a bit more modern before long. That is, if their experiment—Paul's word for their move to the house—didn't prove to be a failure. As yet, she considered, there was no indication either way. It was too soon . . .

Lumas, raising his voice slightly, broke into her reverie:

"So, Mrs. Griffin—"

"Rachel," she interrupted, smiling. "Please call me Rachel." She wondered why she hadn't said that to him long before. Perhaps, she reasoned, she was too enamored of the name—"Mrs. Griffin"—loved the sound of it, the good feeling it gave her.

"Rachel," Lumas went on; he paused briefly, as if tasting the name; a quick smile appeared all over his face—it was replaced by a deep frown, like the caricature of a frown. "That's why I say New York City ain't no place for no one, not even the people that live there and say they like it. They're just kidding themselves." He paused expectantly.

"Yes, of course," Rachel said; she cursed herself for not having listened well enough. "Of course," she repeated. "I fully agree."

"Do ya?" A vaguely condescending grin—ludicrous on the normally gentle face.

"Yes, yes, I do."

"With what?" His grin strengthened, became a sneer. He'd trapped her. And, oddly, he was reveling in it.

Rachel thought of admitting she hadn't listened—it was no big thing. Lumas would merely forgive her and that would be the end of it. "With what you said, Mr. Lumas."

" 'Hank,' I told you that before, Rachel." The words were merely a reminder, not a rebuke.

"Hank."

"That's better. Now, what was we talking about? Oh yeah: You like it here, Rachel? You like this house?"

He was letting her off the hook, Rachel realized. His innate kindness had prevailed. "Yes," she sighed. "And no. I don't like being without a phone. And no windows." She gestured at the boarded-up window at the back of the living room. "It'd be nice to get some light in here. This darkness depresses me." She paused briefly. "And I guess I've grown used to the city—the confusion, the noise, you know. Sounds silly, doesn't it? But I grew up in cities, and this"—she gestured—"is too new an experience for me."

Lumas nodded once, meaningfully. "And a good one, take my word for it, not that you won't find out and agree soon enough. Cities is unnatural. Unnatural."

"Maybe. But you grow used to them in a hurry. Sometimes I think confusion is a part of . . ."

44

Lumas, anticipating her, chuckled gurglingly, as if something were caught in his throat.

"I know," Rachel continued, annoyed but trying not to show it, "that you don't agree with me, Mr. Lumas . . . Hank. And I understand your feelings. I really do. But—" She stopped, uncertain of where to go from there.

"Paul speak to the sheriff about those vandals?" Lumas asked.

Rachel hesitated, not sure that she liked the abrupt way he'd changed the subject.

"You said he was gonna talk to him about it," Lumas went on.

"Yes. He did. Not to anybody's satisfaction, I'm afraid —ours especially. The sheriff said he'd look into it when he got the chance. He seemed to feel it was only some 'neighbor kids.' " She shook her head slowly. " 'Neighbor kids,' can you believe that?"

"So he ain't gonna do nothin'? That's a shame. Catch the bastards that done it you could make 'em pay."

"I suppose. It doesn't matter, really. All that's left is the windows, and those will be in soon enough. And the reshingling"—on the outside of the house. "But that's nearly finished, isn't it?"

"Uh-huh," Lumas said. He glanced around the refurbished room as if for the first time. "Yeah," he said. "We done good work, didn't we?"

Rachel smiled self-consciously: *we*, indeed. The man was being kind again. Or perhaps 'we' referred to Paul and himself, and left her out entirely. If so, it was unfair.

"Yes," she ventured, "we did."

Lumas gave her a broad, toothy smile. The smile vanished abruptly. "Where's that husband of yours?" he asked. "I saw your car out front."

"Oh yes. He's in the woods. He got himself a rifle

and he's gone looking for that wolf, or whatever. He took an ax, too . . ."

"Wolf?" Lumas said. He fell silent for a moment. Rachel looked confusedly at him:

"Yes," she said. "Remember . . . that deer you and Paul found—"

"Oh yeah, right," Lumas stammered. He stood. "I got to be going, Mrs. Griffin. Thanks for your hospitality." He made for the back door. Halfway through the kitchen he yelled, "Thanks again," and, seconds later, he was gone.

Paul took a dozen long steps to the south. Before him lay a clearing filled with skunk cabbage; the huge, tapering oval, pale-veined, almost luminescent green leaves fanning obliquely outward from the center of each plant allowed nothing to grow beneath it. Where there was not skunk cabbage, there was only moist, dark soil.

After a minute, he moved around the southern edge of the clearing and came upon another clearing. Here, years and years of wind and rain had produced a steep and barren incline. Below it, the land had flooded; the few sparse trees protruding from the ankle-deep algae-covered water, and the thin growths of cattail-like weeds gave the area all the appearances of a swamp, as indeed, Paul knew, it would be, in time. He frowned. How eloquently this place spoke of abandonment, and solitude, and melancholy. How unlike all he had grown accustomed to in the past twenty-one years.

Abruptly, he turned away and retraced his steps until the archway became visible again—a small patch of glaring white light against a foreground of gray.

He turned, moved north. Eventually, he came upon a small grove of honey locusts. Several of the trees had fallen victim to weather, and to man, but, as a whole, the grove—impossibly—appeared to be thriving. Paul smiled quickly, spontaneously, as if at the birth of a child, or at the too often postponed marriage of lovers.

Careful of its numerous long thorns, he sat on the nearby trunk of one of the downed trees.

He realized, after a moment, that what he'd thought to be the sounds of birds and small animals were, in reality, the sounds of the trees responding to the gathering wind—leaves turning over and over again; the varied and dismal moanings of the larger trees being moved an inch, two inches, then, as the wind paused, moaning back; the slight crackling sounds at the tops of the shorter trees; the wind itself cooing distantly and evenly, like a flock of pigeons stuck on one long note.

He sensed, more than felt, the hesitant, silent movement that originated at the far end of the honey locust. He looked over; the wind, he saw, was pushing the confusion of dead branches about.

He stood and moved a few feet along the trunk. The trillium was in greater abundance here than in any other part of the forest. There was some ivy snaking through the branches closest to earth, and, on the east side of the trunk, just below where the branches started, a large growth of yellow-brown shelf fungus had established itself. In a large, roughly circular area below the fungus—jutting out of the covering of leaves and pine needles—was a growth of puff-balls. Paul grinned at the word. Whispered it. And bent over for a close look at the one nearest to him. He saw that its color was lighter than he remembered, that it closely resembled the color of his skin. But it was an illusion. The approaching storm had caused the light to change; his hands, his normally blue coveralls, even the gray trunk of the honey locust bore a slightly orange cast. In an effort to shield it from the sickly, all-pervasive light of the coming storm, he cupped his hands over the puffball. Its color altered slightly. He straightened and, unthinkingly, kicked

47

at it. He realized, as his kick landed, that he'd done that same thing years and years before—because the puffballs, bulging with spores, he remembered, exploded delightfully. This one didn't. As he watched, it slowly, grotesquely, lost its shape; first the side that he'd kicked, then the rounded top, then the far sides, as if the weight of some invisible animal was upon it. Finally, it lay at his feet like a crumpled piece of thin discolored leather, and the wind blew bits of long-dead leaves over it.

"C'mon boy!" Paul heard. He turned. Henry Lumas, a look of urgency on his thickly lined face was standing not more than a few yards away. Paul grinned self-consciously. "I was . . ." He pointed at the growth of puffballs. "I remember . . ."

"Never mind that!" Lumas commanded. "There's a hell of a storm coming." He indicated the rifle Paul had set, barrel pointing upward, against the base of the honey locust, and the ax beside it. "Get those and get your ass back to the house."

Paul did as told, feeling—not unpleasantly—like a child again.

I've got some squash and meat cooking and have time to add a few more lines to this letter.

I just took a quick look out the back door and was surprised to see that the sky to the west has become quite threatening. I hope Paul has sense enough to come home soon. It's not that he's particularly careless about his own safety, he just seems to become preoccupied. I remember when he and Mr. Lumas were covering the windows. You haven't been here yet, so you don't know how this house is laid out. It's two stories tall, and Paul and Mr. Lumas had to use this old rickety ladder to get at the second-floor windows. In back, because of the cellar wall, the climb is higher than in the front, and to get at the second-floor windows Paul had to climb nearly to the top of the ladder, where the rungs are rotted and dangerous. Mr. Lumas told Paul a couple times to be careful but—I was watching from inside the second-floor back bedroom, ready to hand him the scrap wood—Paul *flew* up that ladder in his enthusiasm to get the work done. Well, one of the rungs broke in his hands and he nearly fell. After that, he was more cautious. I think *that's* Paul's problem—his enthusiasm. He seems to want so much to put things in order that he temporarily loses track of simple caution.

Rachel put the pen down; the back door had opened, she realized. A moment later, Paul and Lumas appeared in the living room doorway.

"Hi," Paul said. He was grinning stupidly, as if drunk. Lumas, just behind him, scowling, said:

"Wouldn't let this boy out by hisself, if I was you, missus." It was a joking remark, Rachel knew, although, she noted, she would not have been able to tell by his tone.

"Thanks for bringing him home, Hank," she said.

Lumas nodded, still scowling.

"Paul," she went on, "put that thing away. Please." She indicated the rifle Paul held at an awkward angle in his right hand.

Paul glanced at the weapon. "Oh, sorry," he said; he disappeared into the kitchen.

Lumas stepped into the living room, leaned over Rachel, and said, "He don't know much about how things happen around here, does he?"

Rachel stared blankly at the man. "What do you mean, Hank?"

The barest hint of a smile appeared on Lumas' face. "Nothin'," he said. "Never mind. Nothin' at all." He straightened.

Paul reappeared. "Supper almost ready, Rae?" (It was a nickname Rachel merely tolerated; Paul used it only at times such as this—when his maturity was somehow in question, or he thought it was, and he was trying to reestablish it.) He crossed the room and plopped into his winged-back chair.

"In a few minutes," Rachel said. "I put it on about a half hour ago." She glanced at Lumas, indicated her wicker chair. "Sit down, Hank."

"No thanks. I got to be goin'."

"Stay for supper," Paul offered. "We owe you at least that much for all the work you've done."

"You don't owe me nothin'." He paused. "But if you got enough, yeah—I'll stay."

"Good," Paul said. He looked at Rachel. "Hank tell you what we saw on the way back?"

"No, he didn't. What—"

"Nothin' to tell," Lumas cut in sharply. "Paul said he seen somethin'—"

"You've got that backward, don't you?" Paul said. "You pointed it—*him*, I mean—out to me."

"Him?" Rachel asked.

"Or her," Paul amended. "Somebody, at any rate. A child, maybe. It was hard to tell because of the rain."

"The rain?"

"Over in those fields." He gestured to the north. "It was raining there and Hank pointed at this person . . . this kid running away to the north, through the fields. I could hardly see him, but Hank said he was naked; didn't you, Hank?"

Lumas said nothing. He looked as if he felt intimidated.

50

"If it was a child," Paul went on, "we should probably go after him, for his own protection. I mean, if he was naked, as you said, Hank, and he's caught in that storm—"

"Wasn't nothin'," Lumas cut in. "Wasn't nothin' at all. Forget it."

"But we did see—"

"Forget it! Storms and such play tricks on ya. I oughta know. And that's all it was. Just a trick."

Paul looked incredulously at him, then at Rachel. He grinned stupidly again. "Okay, Hank. Whatever you say."

"I'll get the table set," Rachel said, standing. "It's good that you're staying, Hank," she continued.

CHAPTER 7

Paul couldn't believe what Lumas was telling him:

"It's not like they was broke, Paul. I know for a fact they wasn't. But, like I said, that's all they wanted."

Paul leaned over and idly fingered the small, rough-hewn, wooden crosses. "Margaret—1970," he murmured. "Joseph—1971." He looked up at Lumas. "Why," he began incredulously, "didn't they scratch the birthdates in? And the last name? What kind of people were the Schmidts?"

"Can't say I know the answer to that, Paul. They lived here six, seven years. But I was never what you would call close to 'em. They let me work for 'em now and again, but as far as playing cards with 'em, or just sittin' in front of the fire and chewin' the fat—it never happened. They wasn't much for conversation, you know —just work and sleep. And they was awful religious, which is okay, but not for me." He pointed stiffly. "For instance, you know what kind of wood those crosses is made of?"

"Some kind of fruitwood, I imagine," Paul answered.

"Nope. It's dogwood. I can show you the tree they took 'em from." He jerked his head backward to indicate the forest.

Paul straightened. "I don't understand. What's the significance?"

"Can't say what's significant about it. All I know is that the cross they put Christ on was made'a dogwood. That's what I read, Paul. And I'll tell you another thing. Those kids was buried in only a sheet, no box, no nothin'. Just a sheet, and one of those crosses you see people wearin' round their necks . . ."

"A crucifix?" Paul offered.

"That's right. A crucifix. Put one each in their little white hands and then wrapped 'em in the sheet from head to toe, and put 'em in the earth. Kind of godawful way to say good-bye to their own kids, don't you think?" Paul started to answer in the affirmative, but Lumas went on, "What might as well have been their own kids, I mean."

"They weren't, Hank?"

"You never met the Schmidts, Paul?"

"No. My uncle rented the house to them—even after I took ownership . . ."

"That explains it," Lumas cut in. "The Schmidts was about you and your wife's age, a little younger. And these kids here"—he nodded at the wooden crosses—"was ten, twelve years old." He paused meaningfully. "They was adopted. That's what the Schmidts told me. They adopted these kids."

Paul, at Rachel's insistence, left the cat curled up on the winged-back chair and tried to make himself comfortable on the couch. "According to Hank," he explained, "those children were just . . . here, one day. And

53

the Schmidts told him that an orphanage in Syracuse was very happy to find homes for them, they being older—not, you know, babies, infants."

Rachel, in her wicker chair at the opposite end of the room, look quizzically at him. "And they died a year or so later, Paul? What of?"

"The girl—her name was Margaret—of pneumonia, according to what Hank told me. It was very late in the year, there'd been an abrupt change in the weather—very warm one day, very cold the next." He stood, went to the back window, peered out. After a moment, he continued, "There was an ice storm, Hank says, and the little girl got caught in it, in this ice storm. A week later, she was dead."

"How awful," Rachel said. She averted her eyes briefly, as if remembering. "And the Schmidts reacted very . . . coldly to the whole thing?"

"Hank tells me they did, but who knows? I mean, it's difficult to tell, isn't it, how a person is actually reacting at such times. He may appear to be taking things very coldly, very impassively, when, in reality, he's going through hell."

"I don't know, Paul. Hank's very . . . sensitive, despite his appearance. I'm sure you've noticed."

"Yes, I have. But it's hard to square what he's told me with what my own reactions would have been under the same circumstances, though there are these awful wooden crosses, of course. And the fact that the children were buried wrapped only in a sheet, no coffin."

Rachel grimaced. "That's disgusting, Paul."

Paul nodded grimly. A moment's uneasy silence followed, then Rachel continued, "And the boy? What did he die of?"

"No one knows. They called in Dr. what's-his-name

from town, but he just said something about calling in a specialist, and, in the interim, the boy died."

"The boy's name was Joseph?"

"That's what's on his . . . marker, though Hank says he never heard the Schmidts call him that, or the girl 'Margaret.' In fact, all he remembers about the relationship the Schmidts had with those children is that it was *very* quiet. Hardly a word ever passed between them. But that, I think, we can take with a grain of salt. Hank admits not being . . . socially involved with them. That's not the way he put it, of course."

Rachel grinned. "Hank's quite something, isn't he?"

"Uh-huh. Almost the stereotype of your aged, weather-worn hermit."

"All I know," Rachel offered, still grinning, "is that I like him."

And the last day, the day the Schmidt woman threw herself from the second-floor window, followed soon afterward by her husband—those small deaths proved what Lumas had contended all along: Some folks can learn to accept what happens here, and some can't. Some can't shake what the cities do to them. Some believe that man alone, and his cities, do the creating, and if you tell them that man's creations are pale and insignificant by comparison, they wouldn't understand. They'd say, "What do you mean? Tell us what you mean." And you'd know you couldn't tell them. You'd know you might talk for hours but they wouldn't understand, or they'd understand and not believe it. Maybe they'd laugh—the kind of laugh that says, "We *are* superior after all, aren't we?" Then you'd show them they weren't. And they'd stop laughing. Maybe they'd do what the Schmidts did. And you'd have to see to it that their bodies were put back

55

where they belonged. Like the bodies of the children were.

But maybe none of it would happen this time. It had started, but Paul Griffin had a bad destructive streak in him, though he'd deny it. He wanted to put things in order, *his* order, which had nothing to do with what had been intended.

His father had understood right off. And there was hope to be gained from that, because Paul was his father's son. There was hope. For Rachel, too. Maybe more than for Paul. She understood more than she realized.

This is turning out to be quite a long letter, isn't it? A lot longer than I thought it would be.

I've got good news. Friday, the man comes to put in the windows. Thank God! I go outside as much as I can to get away from this lousy darkness (our lights don't help much). Paul's getting the fields ready for next spring's planting (he has to put in a "cover crop" or something), and sometimes I watch him, and other times I go on little nature walks. It's amazing how many kinds and varieties of wildlife there are here, mostly insects and spiders of one sort or another, and birds—cardinals, hawks, etc.

Lately, my walks have been short. That wolf (I find it hard to believe there actually is one) is once again on the prowl. Paul found several more slaughtered animals, woodchucks and such, and a small fox, and early this morning he was awakened by noises outside our bedroom window. He swore he saw something moving around near the barn (about seventy-five feet away), though it was much too dark for him to be certain. Also, the weather has become amazingly unpredictable. We might have gorgeous blue skies early in the day, but by afternoon it can be sullen, and overcast—as it is now. In the last week we've had two vicious storms, and walking anywhere, even on the road in front of the house, can be risky.

Believe me, I'd like to get outside more than I've been able to. Other than its darkness (only temporary), this house is pretty noisy. It's an old house, and noises are to be expected from old houses, I suppose, and maybe in time I'll grow accustomed to its sounds. But—and this is what I don't like—the noises this house makes are even less predictable than the weather. It's as if there's a kind of diminutive symphony orchestra caught in the walls and floors and in the cellar, and one after the other each member of that orchestra wheezes shortly into his brass instrument, or picks at his stringed instrument as if there's something foreign on it, or runs his fingers delicately along his percussion instrument; and, all at once, it will seem that the whole orchestra has decided to go out for lunch, and so they put their instruments down with varying degrees of gentleness and go galumphing, tiptoeing, running out the back door.

The noise of a bad cellist locked up in the cellar have been upstaged by the noise of a healthy rain flinging itself against the house.

Paul will be in shortly.

My love to all,
Rachel

But it wasn't rain, Rachel saw. It was a fitful, strong wind.

She had gone to the back door, had pushed the screen door open, and was waiting for Paul to appear around the corner of the house from the path a hundred yards to the north.

She saw the hawk first as an indefinable speck over the western horizon, over the forest.

A minute later, she could make out the slow, easy movements of its great wings—the wind, she noted, did not appear to be affecting it.

Then it was over the far field, the field Paul had been working for the last two weeks.

"Paul!" she called spontaneously, as if the hawk was a threat to him.

She saw, then, that the hawk was carrying something in its talons—something the size of a small cat—and that the thing was jerking about spastically, like a malfunctioning windup toy.

Then the hawk, its great brown wings still moving slowly, easily, gracefully, was over the near field—and she could hear it screech occasionally, just on the edge of discord.

"Go away," she whispered. Tightly. Desperately. "Go away. Please!"

CHAPTER 8

Ten million deaths happened that day. Most of the deaths went unnoticed, except by those that killed, and those that died. The forest survived because of the dead; the dead were food for the living, and the children and grandchildren of the living.

Near the edge of the forest, a pair of burying beetles had laboriously dug a hole beneath the corpse of a young blue jay. Earlier in the day, a crow in search of food for its young had forced the blue jay from its nest, then had impaled and lost it. Now the burying bettles were busy pushing dirt over the corpse. They did their work quickly, perhaps aware that the longer the corpse remained visible, the greater the chances were that a raccoon or an otter or a fox would come along and snap it up.

From one of the lower branches of an old and insect-hollowed pine, a great horned owl watched the burying beetles. His almost constant hunger had been satisfied. Attached to the back of his neck, by the teeth, was the rapidly putrifying head of a marsh mink. What remained of its body lay in the forest somewhere. The owl had gorged itself on it—once he had been able to separate it from the head—but the jaws of the mink were strong, and its teeth were sharp, even now. In time, the head would fall away.

His powerful back legs holding him fast to the petal tissue of a wild tulip, an ambush bug waited patiently until a fat honeybee settled onto the flower and started the business of pollination. Though the ambush bug was only one-tenth the size of the bee, it attacked, quickly maneuvered it into the correct position, stung it between the eyes, and began its meal. The bee died five minutes later.

The enemies of the snowshoe hare were numerous. Besides the owl and the mink, the fox, and the weasel, they included the ever-present red-tailed hawk. The forest housed six hawks, and one of the hawks could always be seen circling just above the trees. The hare didn't see the one above the clearing until it was nearly upon him, when the time for escape had long since passed.

Near a small pond just beyond the forest's western perimeter, a praying mantis had hidden himself in a growth of cattails. A perfect hunter, the mantis would eat almost anything it could catch. Not far from the mantis, a hummingbird—its wings invisible in the dim, early morning light—floated from flower to flower and finally hovered near a bee balm flower, close to the mantis. The mantis moved forward stealthily, then its powerful legs shot out and quickly reduced the hummingbird to an unrecognizable mass of feathers and flesh.

Near a cluster of sumac, a vixen fed growlingly on the carcass of a woodchuck. Her attention was diverted for a moment by a pair of blue jays flying away from the forest. An hour before, two crows had attacked the jays' nest, and now the gutted bodies of four blue jay chickens lay on the ground beneath. One of the bodies had already been found by a burying beetle. Another burying beetle had since joined it. Together, they would dig a hole beneath the blue jay chicken, then cover it so none of the other thousands of predators would find it.

Time was not measured here. Though it existed.

Life consumed it.

And death consumed it.

But death is only a servant to life—in all its forms; from the amoeba to the dragonfly to the owl and the hawk; from the euglena to the wild tulip to the white pine; from the lady's slipper to the death's cap.

Where sun, and soil, and water combine, there is life.

CHAPTER 9

At first, Rachel took little notice of the footprints. After all, the evidence of someone's bare feet in the newly soaked earth wasn't that unusual. Kids enjoyed that sort of thing—running around with no shoes on, especially after a heavy rain.

Smiling wistfully at the footprints, Rachel set her basket of just-washed clothes on the ground in front of the makeshift clothesline and glanced around at the steep flight of steps leading to the back door of the house. She could dimly see Paul in the far field, the one closest to the forest. When he finished his work, she'd tell him about her near-tumble down the steps; dry rot had made using them precarious, at best. Hopefully, he and Mr. Lumas could fix them soon.

She fished a pair of Paul's long johns from the wicker basket, hung them from the line, and laughed as they flapped crazily in a sudden brisk wind.

This isn't New York City, is it? She stopped laughing abruptly, stood on tiptoes, looked across the fields at Paul: The distance was too great, she realized, and the wind too strong—he'd never hear her. She settled back on her heels. *This isn't New York City, is it?* Paul had told her that during their first night at the house.

She turned. Where had she been, however temporarily?—back in New York, where children were as common a sight as lampposts? Where had she been for those few moments after she'd noticed the footprints?

She studied the bare earth around her. There were no other footprints, only hers and . . . the child's? Yes, without a doubt, she reasoned, a child had made them. They were far smaller than her own footprints, and they were not nearly as deep, but mere soft impressions in the earth, the impression of the heel noticeably shallower than the impression made by the toes. The child had been running, or moving stealthily toward the house.

She bent over and ran her fingers around the perimeter of one of the footprints. The child, she thought, had paused here—the footprint was the same depth all around. She shifted her position slightly. The other print, she saw, was the same. She straightened, pursed her lips. What, she asked herself, was this stupid game she'd involved herself in? The fact was that someone had been prowling around the house. Paul had to be told immediately.

Studying the line of footprints once more—it seemed important to be able to tell Paul what route the intruder had taken—she turned and started for the path that ran along the northern edge of the fields. She stopped and gazed confusedly at the cellar door. Had she seen correctly? Did the small footprints end there—at the door? It would mean that the intruder had gotten into the cellar, but that was impossible—the door was closed and its simple lifting latch was not operable from the inside. Once in the cellar, you had to leave the door open or be trapped behind it. And most importantly, getting the snug-fitting door open even a foot or so—enough to squeeze through into the cellar—was quite a noisy affair, requiring a great deal of strength. If someone had opened it, Rachel knew, she'd have heard the metallic shriek of the hinges, the whine of the door moving against its frame. No, the intruder had merely approached the door, tried it unsuccessfully, then moved north along the cellar wall. His feet would leave no marks in the weeds there.

She turned her head suddenly and cupped her hands to her mouth. "Paul," she called. "Paul!" she repeated, feeling a twinge in her throat. Amazed, relieved, she saw that Paul was looking her way. Several moments later, he had crossed through the field and was loping down the path to the house.

Paul put his ear to the cellar door. Rachel, just behind him, said, "No one could have gotten in there, Paul. I would have heard—"

"Quiet!" Paul hissed. His sudden impatience took Rachel by surprise. She stepped back;

"There's no one *in* there!" she protested.

Paul straightened, firmly grasped the door's wooden handle with his right hand, and opened the latch with his left. He pulled experimentally on the handle. "Jesus," he muttered, "it's going to take two men to get this goddamned door open. It's old wood, the rain must have warped it." He turned his head and looked inquiringly at Rachel. "Have you seen Hank around?" he asked.

Rachel shook her head. "No, I haven't," she answered. "But what does it matter, Paul? There's no one—"

"Yes," Paul cut in, "there is. I can hear him. The poor bastard probably got caught in the rain . . ." He put his ear to the door again. "Hello," he said. "You in the cellar; are you all right? Can you hear me?" He waited a moment, and went on, his voice louder, "Hello, can you *hear* me?" Another pause. "Jesus," he whispered. "Rachel, give me a hand here."

Rachel stepped up to the door and put her hands above Paul's; several seconds later they pulled the door free of its frame. "Okay," Paul said, "I can get it now." Rachel hesitated a moment, then moved to the right where she could peer into the inch-wide opening between the door and the frame. "I can't see anything," she said, and paused. "But I think . . . I can hear him."

The piercing noise of the hinges straining against themselves followed, and Paul had the door open. He let his hands fall to his sides and breathed heavily. "Going to have to . . . get that damned thing . . . fixed," he said.

Rachel hurried about the kitchen: "Have you seen the coffee, Paul?" she asked, throwing a cupboard door shut and opening another.

Paul slowly seated himself at the kitchen table. "I was sure," he mumbled. "I heard him. I *heard* him."

"Here it is," Rachel said.

"And those footprints," Paul went on. "He had to have been in there. Where else could he have been?"

Rachel took the bag of coffee beans to the grinder. "Paul," she said, her tone vaguely condescending, "you searched everywhere, didn't you?" She waited, though it had been a rhetorical question. Paul nodded once. "Well, then," she continued, "the simple fact is—there was no one there, like I said in the first place." She smiled as if to indicate that that was the end of the discussion.

"It was dark," Paul said. "You couldn't tell just *how* dark from outside. Hell, I bumped into that chest of drawers we put down there, it was so dark. The lantern didn't help much. I could have overlooked—"

"How could anyone hide down there?" Rachel interrupted. "Could *you* hide down there?"

"No. But I'm not a child."

"Can we be sure it *was* a child?"

"It was you that suggested it originally. And from the size of those footprints, I don't see how it could have been—"

"I was wrong," Rachel told him. "Very simple."

"No. You weren't wrong. And when Hank shows up, he and I are going to have another look—unless you've overcome your fears of . . . Well, never mind. If there is someone down there, Hank and I will find him."

"I'm sure you will," Rachel said flatly. She poured the coffee beans into the grinder.

Paul inhaled deeply. "I'm sorry," he said on the exhale. "I didn't mean to sound as if I was condemning you. But it really would have helped if you'd come with me."

"And leave the door unguarded? If someone *was* in there he could have snuck out while we were looking for him." She turned the handle of the coffee grinder slowly, methodically.

"Uh-huh," Paul said. "I suppose."

"You think that's just an excuse, don't you?"

He grinned. "Yes." He pointed at the coffee grinder. "You can stop now; I don't want any." He stood abruptly. "I think I'll go looking for Hank."

"This morning," Rachel began, at a whisper, "he said he wasn't feeling well. He's probably in that cabin of his."

"Not feeling well? Why didn't you tell me?"

Rachel shrugged. "I don't know. It slipped my mind."

"Slipped your mind?" He waited a second for the explanation he knew was not forthcoming. "Well," he went on, "did he say what was wrong?"

"No, not really. Stomach pains, I guess."

"Stomach pains?" It was more a statement than a question.

"Yes, nothing serious." She paused. "It's probably that diet of his—"

"There's nothing wrong with his diet," Paul inter-

66

rupted. He crossed the room and opened the back door. "I'll be back in an hour or so. Have dinner ready."

"Yes, okay," Rachel said.

She closed the door behind him.

I've got a few minutes, so I'll add this P.S.

In case you were worried about it—the man's coming to put the windows in on Monday (it's Friday as I write). And that will be the end of *that* experience. It's going to cost quite a bit, of course, but that can't be helped (though I wish the house had been insured).

Also, we've got the car back. Well, we've had it back for a couple weeks, though we haven't used it much. There's a theater in town and I told myself when we first got here that we'd be going out a lot, that we'd be constantly bored. No such luck. We've been working too hard getting this place in shape to get bored. Little things, now, like the back porch steps, and the screens around the front porch, and stripping a coat of ugly brown paint off the floor in here (the living room) to get at the beautiful pine floors beneath. Paul has assigned many of these small jobs to me. Not that I mind. And besides, I've found that when I'm not working I don't get bored. Many people would call it boredom but

Damn I'll be glad when the man comes to put the windows in. I just thought I saw

And now I hear

For several minutes, Rachel stared silently at the child. Sitting on his heels between the refrigerator and the west wall of the kitchen, his torso forward so his chest touched his knees, he was, she realized, trying to hide from her even as she watched—his little side-stepping motions a pathetic attempt, she cringed, to flow into the wall, as if he believed his small body could be made porous, or as if, getting near enough to the wall, he had the power to change his color to its color. And his shallow breathing, she knew, was an effort; every once in a while a low-pitched humming sound came from him, as if he was on the verge of snoring—it was obvious that his body wanted more air than he was allowing it.

Desperately, as she watched him, she wanted to say *Look at me, please!* but couldn't. It would frighten him, disappoint him, spoil his game, she thought, if, by speaking, she gave him proof that she knew he was in the house.

She reconsidered: It was not a game he was playing. Impossibly, he feared for his life, feared her, felt trapped, or suddenly helpless. She couddn't say why these thoughts came to her. Regardless of the dim light, she could see that his face was expressionless; someone seeing a photograph of him would believe he was merely resting, or waiting, or that he was in the middle of a kind of joyless leapfrog.

You should have some clothes on, she wanted to say, but felt, as soon as the words came to her, that it would be a strangely inappropriate remark. He had lived most, perhaps all, of his nine or ten years just as he was now: It was not his dark skin that told her that—but something else. His manner, perhaps, or his quite apparent lack of shame. She thought about that briefly; but it was not apparent, she concluded. None of what she'd so quickly assumed about him was apparent—only imaginative guesses. *He is some wild creature that has gotten into the house, and the only thing human about him is his form.* That is what had come to her the second she'd seen him, she told herself. And it was wrong.

"Wait there," she said.

His body twitched slightly.

"Oh, wait there. Please!" And she backed away from him a few feet and switched on the overhead lamp.

She gasped audibly.

He had turned his head to look at her.

One word—"beautiful"—came to her in that moment. And in the next moment she rejected it. It was not merely inadequate. It was dishonest. Dishonest to herself. To her whole being. Because so much that is commonplace is called beautiful. Men and women are beautiful. And children. And animals. Poetry. Joy. Love. Even sadness. The face she studied—the eyes that studied her—was not.

It was hideous. As perfection has to be. And hypnotic, as the full moon is hypnotic.

A face in total harmony with itself.

For one insane second, she thought that her own children—if there were to be any—would look very much like this child.

The color of his skin was much the same as hers, wasn't it? No, perhaps more like Paul's. And the tapering oval shape of his eyes. Paul's eyes. And the strong chin—Paul had a strong chin. The thought dissipated, victim of her inherent honesty. And of her fear, her confusion.

Her own children, she knew, would be to this child what an Audubon print is to what it depicts. An imitation. Her breathing halted on the word. Had she actually thought it? Meant it?

She took a step closer to the child. He raised his head slightly to keep his eyes on hers.

She had seen that fragile blue—the color of his eyes—before; it was the color of a cloudless early morning sky, just before sunrise, just after all but the brightest stars have gone out. That fragile, pale, and transient blue. A blue so sharply, exquisitely, in contrast to the dark, smooth, almost earth-colored skin.

69

But is was his hair that was earth-colored, she amended. As if the thick, great mass of it falling to his shoulder blades and to the base of his neck—though, curiously, not over his forehead—was a strange kind of rich topsoil.

The high cheekbones and straight nose were reminiscent of the American Indian, she thought, but not, her thoughts continued, so stark as that—more as if the smooth, flawless, dark skin covered, not bone and cartilage, but something far less substantial; clay, perhaps. Soft clay.

Above the pale blue eyes, the brows were the same rich topsoil color as his hair, and just as thick and full, but they did not meet in the middle as such brows so often did; instead, as full as they were, they tapered nearly to a point just over the upper inside edge of the eye sockets. On any other child, the effect would have been ludicrous—as if the child had been fooling around with makeup and tweezers.

His mouth, parted a little, was what some would call a classic mouth—bottom lip full, top lip slightly less full, the two parts forming a dark red, moist unity, and more than that—Rachel's consciousness reeled at the feeling—an invitation. A seduction in and of themselves.

She took a step backward.

As she did so, two things happened at the same time. The overhead lamp flickered once, shot out the deep, harsh blue light that signaled the death of the bulb; darkness re-entered the room.

And the back door opened.

Paul appeared.

"I don't know where Hank is," he said, stooping over to remove his mud-caked boots. "He's not in his cabin. I nearly broke his door down pounding on it." He paused briefly. "Turn the light on, would you, Rachel."

She pointed stiffly, tremblingly, silently, at the child.

"Is something wrong?" Paul asked.

70

She nodded once, sharply, in the direction she was pointing. As she did so, the child put his head between his knees, his squatting position became more severe. "I see you," she blurted. "I see you. You won't get away."

"What the . . ." Paul whispered. Still wearing his right boot, he took a few awkward steps toward the child. "Come out of there!" he ordered.

Rachel looked frantically at her husband. "Don't just stand there, Paul. Get hold of him before . . ." And she knew how utterly foolish that would sound.

Paul hesitated, his gaze first on the child, then on Rachel.

"*Do* something, Paul!"

"Rachel, I . . ." He realized, suddenly, the illogic of what he saw on his wife's face. He had seen that look before, when they had discovered what had been done to the house, and again when he'd told her how Margaret and Joseph Schmidt had been buried: "That's disgusting, Paul," she'd said, and her face had registered that disgust, just as it did now. But now it was far more powerful. Now she was not merely disgusted. She was at the point of revulsion, as if she pointed so stiffly not at a small, naked, dark-skinned, and terribly frightened boy, but at something so grotesque that words to describe it piled up at the back of her tongue and went unspoken because they were inadequate. For one awful moment, he thought he would have to defend the child from her.

His booted foot thudding softly on the oak floor, he took the remaining few steps, leaned over, and put his hands under the child's arms to raise him. The child shuddered violently, as if overcome by a sudden, deep chill. Paul straightened abruptly; "Stop that!" he ordered. He leaned over again and, convinced that the child was not going to uncoil from his fetal position, slipped his left hand around the child's buttocks, the other hand around his

71

knees, and lifted. The child shuddered again, as violently as before, but did not change his position.

"He's light as a feather," Paul said, and carried him into the living room and put him on the couch.

Henry Lumas knew what was happening to him, and it was not that he wanted it to happen. He would have gladly chosen another twenty years or so of life, if it had been offered. But it hadn't. And his seventy-two years had been more good than bad, so he had no real complaints. A few days of pain—from which, a year ago, he remembered, he could have separated himself; but that required the kind of energy he no longer possessed—and it would be over. It would be far easier, he mused, without the pain.

He gazed as lovingly as his pain allowed at the faded snapshot on the crude oak table near his bed. It would be far easier, too, if she were alive and could help him through it, just as he had helped her through it so many years before. Just as he had made her death more joyous for her than it otherwise would have been.

Sam Griffin could have helped him, as well. God, but if that man's death had been just a bit slower—there could have been some comfort for him, some reassurance.

But there was no one, yet. In a month, perhaps a little less. But not yet. The Griffins, Paul especially, would be of no help. All they'd be able to offer was a lot of sympathy and endless pleas that he go to the doctor in town, which would make the whole thing unbearable.

He sat heavily, hand clutched to his stomach, on the bed. He groaned a curse. How long, he wondered, before his fears—which never went away entirely—started chipping away at what he knew? An hour? A day? Or would they wait until his last minutes, or seconds, and then torment him?

Fighting what his body told him, he stood and half stumbled, half walked to the door. It was partway open, he saw: Paul had knocked hard on it. He unhooked the strand of leather that served as a lock and pulled the door open.

Beyond the rise, near the grove of honey locusts—where, he remembered, he had found Paul—there was reassurance, and comfort, as much as any human could give. And he needed it.

CHAPTER 10

"Relax," Paul coaxed. He thought of placing his hand comfortingly on the child's shoulder, but decided against it; how comforting could his touch be, he reasoned, if it caused such a violent reaction in the child?

He turned his head and looked at Rachel. She was standing, her face coldly expressionless, at the other end of the couch. "Get a blanket, would you, darling," he said.

Rachel hesitated a second, then nodded slightly to indicate the child. "See if you can get him to lie down, Paul. That position he's in . . . it's grotesque."

"Grotesque?"

"Yes, it's unnatural."

"Painful is probably a better word," Paul said dryly.

He put his hands on the child's arms; "Come on now, young man"—gently, as if talking to a child several years younger—"why don't you lie down . . ." He realized that his touch had sparked no reaction; it was a good sign, he thought. "Lie down here." He found the child responding to the very soft pressure of his hands. "That's right." He looked at Rachel again. "Are you going to get that blanket?" She started for the bedroom. "Turn that lamp on, too," Paul continued; he nodded at a wrought-iron, floor-standing lamp—it was minus a shade—to the right of the couch, near the bedroom doorway. "I can hardly see a thing." He paused. "And don't be so glum."

He succeeded in coaxing the child onto his side, though not out of his fetal position. "That's good, young man; now straighten your legs." He rolled the child onto his back and put pressure on his knees. "Loosen up . . . there, that's the way." The child allowed Paul to straighten his legs so he was in a sitting position, but with his head just above his knees and tightly clenched fists pressed to his ears. "Loosen up," Paul repeated. "No one wants to hurt you." He put his hands on the child's shoulders and eased him back.

Rachel appeared from the bedroom. "Here's the blanket," she said, her words measured, stiffly casual. She laid the blanket at the child's feet, then switched on the floor-standing lamp. Nothing. "Bulb must be dead." she muttered.

"Or it's that goddamned generator," Paul said. He nodded toward the kitchen. "Get one of those kerosene lamps from the closet in there."

Saying nothing, Rachel went into the kitchen.

The child was in a prone position, his fists still clenched at his ears. Paul grasped his wrists and gently pulled forward until the child's arms were straight; "There" —smiling benevolently—"that's better, isn't it?"

Suddenly, the child's body, and Paul's hands—still on the child's wrists—assumed an anemic yellow cast. Paul turned his head sharply: Rachel was just behind him, lantern dangling from her hand. Paul sighed. "You scared me, Rae," he said, and he grinned self-consciously.

"Here's the lamp." She attempted to hand it to him.

"No, no. Bring that table over and put the lamp on

it." He indicated a small, dark wood table between the back windows.

Rachel took several slow steps to her left, the small, rough circle of lamplight moving up the child's body as she moved.

She stopped abruptly. "Paul!"

He looked where she was looking, then looked back at her. "What's the matter?"

"Can't you see? Isn't it obvious?"

"Isn't *what* obvious, Rachel?"

"His face, Paul. Look at it!"

"I did." He looked briefly, again, at the child's face. "I don't understand."

"You don't understand?" Incredulously. "Are you blind, Paul? Can't you see what he is?"

"What in hell are you talking about, Rachel?" He stood and tried to take the lantern from her. She backed away from him, hesitated a moment, and, lantern in hand, ran into the kitchen.

Paul followed a moment later.

She had seated herself at the kitchen table, had buried her face in her hands. The lantern was on the table in front of her—in its light, Paul saw that she was trembling.

"Rachel, please . . ." He pulled a chair away from the table and sat beside her. "Please, darling . . . Are you crying?"

Silence.

"There's no reason to cry, Rachel."

"Get Mr. Lumas." A hoarse whisper. "He'll know what to do. He'll understand." She laid her hands flat on the table, the lamp between them. Paul could see moisture around her eyes and on her cheeks. "He'll know what to do," she repeated aloud, and evenly.

"No," Paul said softly, his hand caressing her cheek.

76

"I think what we need is a doctor, both for the child . . ." He hesitated. "And for you. You've gotten yourself all worked up, and apparently for no better reason than we've found this poor, lost boy—"

She chuckled shortly, hollowly. "You *don't* understand, do you?" She pushed herself away from the table. "Well," she went on, "if you're not going to do anything, then I will." She prepared to stand. Paul put his hand on her arm, stopped her.

"No," he said impatiently. "I don't understand. And I fail to see what Lumas has to do with any of this. It's none of his business, and even if it was, I wouldn't go prowling around in that damned forest looking for him now. It'll be dark in a half hour."

Rachel stood abruptly and went to the back door. "Then you'll have to be quick about it, Paul." She pulled on the doorknob. The door opened an inch. She closed it, unlatched it, and pulled it open again. "I'm serious, Paul."

Paul's jaw dropped. "Jesus," he muttered. "What a fool I've been." Finally, it had come to him. Lumas' door had been locked from the inside; it had opened only slightly in reaction to his heavy knocking. "Throw me my boots." he ordered. "Quick!"

Rachel, surprised by his sudden change of mood, did as asked.

"There's no time to explain, darling," Paul said, slipping his boots on, standing and retrieving his coat from the coat tree near the table. "Just keep your eye on that child. I don't know when I'll be back." He pushed the screen door open and took the back steps three at a time.

Henry Lumas grinned. It was happening—and even more quickly than when the Schmidts lived at the house. Only days now, not weeks. By Saturday, or Sunday at the latest, the earth would set free what she had been clutching

77

to herself these past five years. And in the few days remaining to him perhaps he would be able to prepare the Griffins for the inevitable, get their thinking turned around, *show* them that creation meant more than motorcars and cities and telephone poles. He'd be dead before they understood fully, he knew that; he'd been months trying to make the Schmidts understand and, at last, it hadn't worked. Their fears had been too strong, their ideas of what should be, and of what can be, greater than their ability to accept what *was*.

Paul and Rachel might react the same way, but it was more likely they wouldn't. Rachel possessed a special kind of awareness—with effort she could pass it on to her husband. And if he—Lumas—was there to help . . .

He doubled over suddenly, pain ripping sideways across his stomach and chest, and went down on his knees. In the next moment, he sensed he was falling forward. He reached out to steady himself against the trunk of the dead honey locust.

The sound of human agony is a mixture of fear and confusion and, underlying it, a spontaneous, unspoken plea that the cause of the suffering be ended. An unmistakeable sound. And Paul Griffin, breathless from his run down the rutted path, tensed himself, hearing it, and listened a few seconds, head cocked to one side, for a repeat of the sound. There was none.

"Hank?" he called. "Hank?" he called again, hands cupped around his mouth.

There was no reply.

He stepped carelessly across the brook that separated him from the forest's eastern perimeter. "Hank?!" He lifted his foot out of the soft mud at the brook's edge, listened, heard only the sound of water trickling into the elongated hole his foot had created.

"Hank! It's me, Paul Griffin."

To the south, a grouse hurried into the shelter of some thickets. Ahead, from the lower branches of a huge sycamore, a gray squirrel, obviously annoyed, chattered briefly, and disappeared around the other side.

"Jesus," Paul muttered. "Hank!" he shouted. "Where are you?"

Silence.

He moved quickly up the shallow slope, stopped, and glanced around at the house. He found himself momentarily startled by the fact that, only with effort, could he distinguish it from the land surrounding it. The top edge of the stone roof—dull red because of the setting sun—was clearly visible, but it was not sufficient to immediately suggest that a house lay beneath it. The normally bright green shingles—so cheerful in daylight—now were muted, now blended almost perfectly with the flat near-darkness of the fields, the thickets, and the scatterings of trees. It was a vaguely disorienting sight; Paul turned quickly from it and moved cautiously into the forest.

"Hank?" he called. "Where are you?"

Several minutes later, after stumbling occasionally over darkness-obscured roots and vines, he heard a gurgling, low-pitched moan and plunged mindlessly forward toward what he now knew was its source—the small grove of honey locusts he'd paused at a month before. The grove of honey locusts that Lumas—in what Paul realized, in retrospect, was a fit of temper—had ordered him away from, as if he had been some nameless trespasser bent on the destruction of private, and valuable, property.

Rachel's brow furrowed in confusion. She had known something about this child sleeping so very quietly on the old couch. No, she reconsidered, she had not merely known *something* about him—his exact age, for instance—she had known *everything*. But just briefly. A few minutes at most —not long enough that the knowledge had implanted itself on her consciousness, not long enough that it was anything more, now, than a dim, elusive feeling she could appreciate for only a small fraction of a second. And that feeling, as weak as it was, was growing weaker by the minute.

Why, for instance, had she told Paul that Henry Lumas would "understand"? Understand what? Was the child his? But that was silly. If Lumas understood, it was an understanding identical to what she had experienced only a half hour before. An understanding, a feeling, which, for her, would soon be gone entirely, like the lingering, then static, then irrecallable aura of a particularly distasteful dream.

She had acted as if in a panic, she remembered. She had pointed stiffly at the child and pleaded, "Get hold of him, before . . ." Before what? Did she suppose that he could walk through walls?

And a minute or two later, as Paul prepared to look the child over, when the lamplight had fallen on the child's face—what had she seen there that had caused her to run, frightened, into the kitchen and bring her to the point of tears? There was nothing in the child's face to cause such a reaction. It was a perfect face. As perfect, she thought, as the face of a wild flower.

"Damn!" she whispered tightly, more in frustration than anger.

She rose from her wicker chair, went into the kitchen, to the back door. She opened it and peered into the soft, nearly liquid darkness beyond. It was a harder, heavier darkness at the horizon: Paul was there—in the midst of that darkness. He had vaulted into it from the shelter of the house. But why? Was something wrong with Lumas? Obviously, Paul knew something he was not telling her— hadn't had the time to tell her, she corrected. Because this was the first time since he and Lumas had discovered the ravaged deer that he had left the house after sunset. It had to be true—Henry Lumas was ill and needed Paul's help. And Paul, apparently unmindful of the very real danger to himself, was going to give it. Paul must care a great deal about the old man, she thought. Perhaps, with his stories about living alone in those woods, and his intense hatred of *"civilization,"* Lumas reminded Paul of Paul's father— albeit, not in a physical way. From what Paul had said about his father, there was certainly no physical resemblance. But such things actually counted for very little. You had to look beyond the eyes and the structure of the face to really know a person. Just as, her thoughts continued, she had done upon encountering the child. She caught herself on the thought. She had seen very little of the child's physical makeup then. She had almost sensed his presence more than been visually aware of it, she realized. And that was when she'd known, however briefly, all there was to know about him. Later, the yellow lamplight on him, it had been the grotesque perfection, the inhuman *symmetry,* of his face that had caused her to run from him; it had harshly confirmed what had, moments before, been a subliminal thing.

She closed the door, wandered into the living room, and stood by the couch, her gaze on the child. He was sleeping, she supposed. His large, oval, pale blue eyes were lightly closed, his firmly muscled chest—how like a man's it was, except that it was totally without hair—moved only slightly, almost imperceptibly, his rhythmic breathing incredibly shallow. His body, Rachel saw, was in precisely the same position Paul had forced it into a half hour . . . no, forty-five minutes before.

She noticed the blanket folded at the child's feet and chided herself for not having the good sense to cover him. She unfolded the blanket and brought it slowly up over his ankles, over his knees, over his thighs. She paused. Yes, she thought, how like a miniature man he was—a miniature, yet strongly developed man whose body bore no traces of hair, except lightly, on the forearms, and lavishly, on the head, but nowhere else, not even around . . . She quickly finished covering him, stepped back, and stared silently, wonderingly, at him for a minute.

"Where did you come from?" she whispered softly. She grinned. The words, she remembered, were part of a poem she'd learned as a child:

"Where did you come from, baby dear?" she said aloud. "Out of the everywhere, into here?"

CHAPTER 11

It was past ten when Rachel, trying unsuccessfully to nap in the wicker chair, heard footfalls on the back steps. *Paul*, she realized. But he was moving so slowly, so heavily, as if in pain.

"Rachel," he called, "open the door."

Rachel bolted from her chair. "Paul?" she yelled as she ran through the kitchen. "What's wrong?" She threw the back door open.

Paul, on the landing now, grinned feebly. "Give me a hand, would you?" he said.

In the dim light, Rachel couldn't see who it was that Paul carried, fireman style, on his shoulders. But she knew that it was Lumas. She hesitated a moment, confused, then—as Paul stepped awkwardly to the right—she pushed the screen door open. Paul moved past her, into the kitchen, and looked about anxiously. He nodded at the table. "Clear that off, Rachel."

"Paul . . . is he . . ."

"No. He's not dead. Just clear the table off."

"Our bed, Paul. Put him on our bed." She hurried

past him into the living room, stopped, looked back. "Well?"

"Yes," Paul said. "Of course." Stepping sideways through the narrow doorway, he followed Rachel into the living room and hesitated briefly beside the couch. He nodded to his left. "How's the boy?"

"Asleep," Rachel answered quickly, "ever since you left."

"Good. That's good."

He followed Rachel into the bedroom and quickly scanned the bed. "Get the cat off it, Rachel," he ordered.

Rachel pushed at the cat's flank a couple of times. "C'mon, Higgins," she said, "shoo." Meowing in protest, the cat moved slowly off the bed.

Paul shifted Lumas' body around so that he carried it for a second in his outstretched arms, then carefully lowered it onto the bed. He straightened, inhaled deeply: "My God"—on the exhale—"I don't ever want to go through *that* again."

"What's wrong with him, Paul?"

"Damned if I know." He inhaled deeply again and knelt on one knee beside the bed. Rachel switched on the lamp on the dresser. It didn't work. "It's that lousy generator," Paul told her. "Just get that kerosene lamp, okay. And some cloth for a bandage." Rachel nodded and went into the living room.

Paul took hold of Lumas' left hand and tried to study it. "Can't see a goddamned thing," he murmured. "Rachel," he called, "the lamp!"

"I'm trying to find a bandage, Paul," she answered peevishly.

"Well, bring me the lamp first."

"How am I going to find a bandage in the dark?"

"For God's sake, we've got more than one lamp in this house."

84

"I'll only be a second . . ." She rummaged about in the medicine cabinet in the bathroom. "Here's one," she called. A moment later she reappeared in the bedroom doorway, lantern dangling from one hand, a white strip of cloth from the other. She held the lantern out. "Here," she said.

"No, hold it over him."

She moved closer to the bed and held the lamp over Lumas.

"That's right," Paul continued. "Now, give me that bandage."

She handed him the bandage. He glanced at her; Lumas' left hand was cradled in his hand. "Pretty messy, huh?" he said.

The muscles of Rachel's face tightened. "What . . . happened to it, Paul?"

"He put a thorn through it," Paul told her.

"A thorn?"

"From a honey locust." He began to wrap Lumas' still-bleeding hand with a bandage.

"What's a honey locust?" Rachel asked.

"It's a tree . . . a tree with thorns on it."

"Oh," Rachel whispered. "Like a rosebush."

Paul glanced quizzically at her. "Yes," he said, "like a rosebush." He tied the bandage into a knot over Lumas' palm and studied the results of his work. "This is no good," he said. "His hand's still bleeding. Don't we have anything else, some cotton or something?"

"Let me do it," Rachel said. She handed him the lamp. "You've got that bandage all wrong. And you've got to clean the wound first."

Paul stared blankly at her a few seconds, as if he intended to give her an argument. He straightened. "I'll get a pan of water," he offered. He stepped away from the bed.

"Yes, good," Rachel said. She leaned over Lumas. "And see if you can find another strip of cloth and a thin piece of wood so I can fix a tourniquet. He seems to have lost a lot of blood, Paul. Has he been bleeding ever since you found him?"

"No. I helped him back to his cabin. He appeared to be okay for a while. We talked—I'll tell you about it—and then, all of a sudden, he was out. His hand must have started bleeding again because of the way I was carrying him."

"Yes," Rachel said, picking at the tight knot Paul had tied in the bandage, "that's possible."

Paul leaned forward in his winged-back chair: "That's the whole story, Rachel. If you make any sense of it, I wish you'd share it with me. He said you'd understand."

"Is that what he said?" A rhetorical question.

"Not in so many words," Paul answered. "He thinks quite a lot of you, Rachel. You should be flattered."

She attempted a smile. "He gives me more credit than I deserve, Paul. He makes me feel like I can't help but disappoint him. If I do have some sort of gift, as he thinks, it's not very . . . dependable."

"What do you mean, darling?"

She averted her eyes a moment. "I don't know," she said. "I don't know. I guess it's just a matter of knowing something one moment, then forgetting it the next moment."

"Something?"

"That's the best I can do, Paul. I can't tell you what I don't know. I'm sorry."

Paul raised his eyebrows; confusion mixed with a gentle admonishment. He felt, Rachel was sure, that she was hiding something from him.

86

"Uh-huh," he said. "This is all getting very cryptic, isn't it? Well, never mind. Lumas"—he nodded toward the bedroom—"thinks he's dying, as I said. And he may be right, for all we know. So anything he says I guess we can chalk up to that—to this feeling of his that he's dying."

"Do *you* think he's dying, Paul?"

"I don't know. I'm not a doctor, am I? But he's been coughing up blood, well . . . you saw that, didn't you?" She grimaced. "It looks like tuberculosis, or an ulcer maybe, and fairly well advanced." He turned his head sharply to the left, his gaze on the darkened bedroom doorway. He put his hands on the arms of the chair and prepared to stand. "Hank?" he called. "Stay in bed, Hank. For God's sake, you're in no condition . . ." He stood, grabbed the kerosene lamp from the table beside the chair, and held it out so its light fell dimly into the bedroom. He saw that Hank was sitting up on the bed. "Hank, lie down—you need to rest." Lumas stood very slowly, right hand to his stomach, the other hand against the bedpost.

"Hank, for Christ's sake!" Paul stammered. Out of the corner of his eye he saw slight movement on the couch. He looked. The child's eyes had opened.

Hank appeared in the bedroom doorway, his right hand still clutching his stomach. "Hank," Paul said, "please . . . go back to bed, you're a very sick man." He took a few quick steps toward him, stopped and saw to his left that the child had thrown the blanket to the floor. "Rachel"—he glanced at her—"cover him, would you?" Nodding, Rachel stood abruptly, went over to the couch, and stooped over to pick up the blanket.

"Leave him be, missus!" Lumas commanded, his voice full and powerful. Rachel looked up at him, then at her husband. "Paul?" she pleaded.

"Cover him, Rachel."

"Leave him be!" Lumas repeated. A hint of violence had been added to the overwhelming power of his voice.

Rachel nervously straightened the blanket and looked confusedly at her husband. "Paul . . . What should I do?"

Trying to establish authority not only over the child, and over Rachel, but over Lumas as well, Paul, his voice cracking, shouted, "Cover him, for Christ's sake!"

Lumas' movements were impossibly quick. In a second he was above the child; in the next second his huge hands encircled the child's throat. For an instant, from opposite vantage points, Paul and Rachel watched a trembling, surrealistic tableau—blue veins bulging on the back of the old man's hands, and the firm muscles and blue arteries of the child's neck bulging above them.

Then Paul, lantern still in his right hand, threw his left arm around the man's throat and pulled. "Hank! Jesus Christ!" he hissed. "Let go, let go!" But the man's strength was immense. Paul held the lantern in back of him. "Rachel, take this!" Rachel dropped the blanket and took the lantern from him. Paul threw his freed arm around Lumas' chest, planted his feet firmly on the floor, pulled hard. "Rachel," he shouted. "His hands. Get his hands!" But before Rachel could act, Paul broke the man's grip on the child and the two of them—Paul and Lumas— fell backward to the floor.

In the moment's silence that followed, Paul knew that one of his ribs had been cracked, or broken. A lower rib, he reasoned—his sudden, panicked breathing was agony. "Rachel," he moaned, "get him off!" But, he realized in the next moment, Lumas was already on his feet and was pointing, as stiffly as Rachel had, at the child still sitting up on the old couch—his perfect, dark face waxy, expressionless.

And from the floor, Paul could see Lumas' nostrils flaring, his arms quivering, the great mound of white hair falling over his blood-caked shirt. "You go back!" the man shouted. "You go back!" Each word an abominable, gurgle-filled gasp.

Seconds later, Lumas turned, crossed through the kitchen, and fled out the back door.

CHAPTER 12

Paul was tired, his ribs were bothering him, he was not, Rachel knew, in the mood for talk. Especially for the kind of talk they had almost pointedly avoided for the past week. It had been easy enough to avoid it. Paul would complain that his ribs hurt, he didn't feel like talking when his ribs hurt, that he'd rather do some reading. And Rachel, after a feeble protest, would accept that. Or he would find some small chore to perform when they were in the same room and talk seemed imminent. He had finished putting new screens around the front porch, had sanded down and rehung the cellar door—with Rachel's help—had begun work on patching up the back steps, had torn apart and rebuilt the generator, hoping that would effect a repair; it hadn't.

The silence, Rachel thought, had begun at the doctor's office a week before. No, she amended—it had actually begun before that, when they had pulled away from the house and Paul, sitting stiffly in the passenger seat, left hand pressed hard to his rib cage, had asked, "The boy upstairs?"

"Yes, in the back bedroom," she'd answered. "The door's locked."

"Good," he'd said.

That had been the beginning of it, she reasoned—the beginning of their silence.

Later, in the doctor's examination room, it had grown more profound: "How did this happen?" the man asked. "You've got a couple cracked ribs there."

And Paul, too quickly, had answered, "I fell. Off our back steps."

Rachel had thought only briefly of contradicting him, but not as if she *intended* to, as if it would be the right thing, the correct thing, to do, but because the truth had already settled in, and she had been mentally toying with it.

Just as she had been doing for the last, silent week.

Paul, too, she realized, had been toying with the truth—had been turning it over, had been examining it from all angles, had been trying hard to accept it.

Had he accepted it? she wanted to know. And, if he had, was it the same truth she grappled with?

"Paul?" she said.

He lowered himself heavily, painfully, into his winged-back chair. "Got to get a new regulator for that damned thing," he said, referring to the generator he'd just coerced—with various obscenities and fumblings with a screwdriver and hammer—into noisy and unsteady life. "Going to keep blowing light bulbs out if we don't get a new regulator," he continued.

"Can we get one in town?" Rachel asked.

"I suppose so. Yeah."

"Well, then . . ."

"All in its own good time, Rachel. All in its own good time."

Rachel took a deep breath. "Why, Paul?"

"Why? Why what?"

"Why 'All in its own good time'?"

"I don't think I understand."

She sighed. "Only because you don't *want* to understand."

An obviously forced chuckle came from him, then stopped abruptly. He put his hand to his ribs. "Jesus," he muttered. He glanced toward the bedroom. "I'm going to lie down for a while. My ribs feel better when I lie down." He prepared to stand.

"Please don't," Rachel said crisply.

He pretended a dumbfounded look. "Oh, I understand—you like to see me in pain."

"Of course not."

"Well, then, you'll let me go lie down, won't you?!"

"Paul, I . . ." She stopped, obviously uncertain of how to continue.

"Yes?" Paul coaxed.

"I think we have to talk."

"I'd rather go to bed."

"I know it. And that's what we've got to talk about."

Paul grinned at that.

"You know," Rachel said, "what I mean. Stop playing—"

"I'm not sure *you* know what you mean, Rae." He stood, more abruptly than she thought he could. "You want to talk about the boy, don't you?"

She hesitated only a moment before answering. "There are a couple things we have to talk about: Mr. Lumas, for instance—"

"He can take care of himself," Paul snapped. "He's done it well enough all these years, he doesn't need us."

"You seem very sure of that, Paul."

"Listen," he sighed, "I saw him early yesterday morning, when I was out fixing the steps, and he seemed fine. Okay?"

"Where? Where did you see him? Did you talk to him?"

"As if I really want to—you seem to forget, Rachel, what that man did. You want to talk to him—you go right ahead. But as far as I'm concerned—"

"So you didn't talk to him?"

"I *saw* him. From a distance. He seemed fine, just fine. Now—may I please go lie down?"

"And what about the boy, Paul?"

He sighed heavily. "We've been over it and over it, Rachel; the boy—"

"Over it and over it? What in hell are you talking about, Paul? We've hardly even . . ."

"He's *your* responsibility. I've got myself to worry about, I thought we discussed that."

"*My* responsibility? I can't believe you actually said that, Paul. If anything, he's *our* responsibility, I don't know . . . the state's responsibility. We can't just—"

"Well, it seems that that's what we're doing, Rachel."

Silence.

"Oh, c'mon, darling," he continued. "You know very well why we've kept him this long. It's that goddamned road; fucking thing's impassable in all the rain we've been having." He smiled feebly, as if at the punch line of an unfunny joke. "As soon as the weather clears—"

"Paul, we're kidding ourselves. That child . . . that child has done something to us . . . he's—he's." She stopped, unsure of how to continue.

Paul said nothing for a moment, seemed to be weighing her words, devising a response. "Oh?" he said. "*What* has the child *done* to us."

"You bastard!" she hissed.

93

"Precisely," he said, smiling again. "Now, may I please go lie down?"

She said nothing.

It was a small square room, "claustrophobic," Rachel called it, with a low ceiling, and walls that had once been white but which had been turned a bilious yellow by time and weather.

Over the years, the afternoon sun through the one, narrow window in the middle of the west wall had left its long, dark, rectangular imprint on the pine floor. Now the window—like the east-facing window in the front bedroom—was boarded up: "We'll wait on that," Paul had told the glazier the previous Monday. "We're not going to be using these rooms anyway." The glazier, though obviously skeptical, had given no argument.

And so the room would have been dark had it not been for the bare low-wattage bulb in the middle of the ceiling; trailing diagonally from the bulb to the northeast corner of the room and from there to a small hole in the floor was a length of brown electrical cord; Paul had installed the bulb when he and Rachel had concluded that leaving a kerosene lamp in the room would be foolish, at best.

And besides, Rachel had pointed out, there was the child to consider. How much he seemed to crave what little sunlight filtered into the room through openings between the boards on the window. The feeble artificial light Paul had provided was no substitute, of course, but, for the moment, it would have to do.

Paul had also put a small folding cot against the south wall. Rachel, hoping to cheer the room up, had covered its mattress with a bright pink sheet; the top sheet and pillow case matched it. And because the combination of bilious yellow walls and bright pink sheets had been, as Rachel termed it, "nauseating," she had, in an attempt to balance the colors off, hung an old print—a landscape; green predominated—in an ornate white frame several feet above the bed. Neither she nor Paul had commented on the effect it produced.

What remained of a four-drawer cherry-wood dresser —minus its smashed mirror—had been placed against the north wall, near the door; only its top drawer had been left intact. It was enough.

The child, prone on the cot, arms at his sides, long thin fingers outstretched, was naked, as Rachel had first found him, as the torn shirt and pants in the dresser drawer proved he wanted to be. The pink top sheet lay crumpled on the floor in front of the cot.

Rachel, thinking the child was asleep, stepped quietly into the room. She had found that, if he was asleep, the slightest noise would wake him. Consequently, because of all the noises the house made, he had gotten—at most, she thought—the equivalent of a full night's sleep in the last seven days.

But he was awake. His eyes were wide open, focused, Rachel supposed, on the ceiling.

But, seeing this, she again experienced what she had experienced several times before: Regardless of the direction of his gaze, she felt certain he was watching her. As if waiting. As if weighing her intentions.

"I've brought you some food," she said. She sounded strained, nervous, she thought, and that always seemed to make the boy nervous. She forced herself to smile. "Are you hungry?" *Yes, that's better.*

She held out the tray she carried. On it was a plate filled with meat loaf and peas, and half a glass of milk.

"It's not bad," she continued. "The meat loaf's a little bland, maybe. But you've got to remember I've only been cooking a short while."

You're being an ass, she told herself.

"I'll leave it right here," she went on, still smiling. She set the tray on top of the dresser. "And when you feel like eating . . ." She hesitated. "This is a fork," she said, holding it up in front of her face. "I've shown you how to use it." She dipped it into the meat loaf. "Like this." She brought it slowly to her mouth, made exagerrated chewing motions. "Do you understand?"

Silence.

"I really think it's important that you understand." She hesitated, set the fork on the tray. "You may talk anytime you feel like it. Paul and I have been waiting . . ."

She found, suddenly, that her eyes had been following the strongly muscled contours of his body—that her gaze had paused admiringly at his legs, his chest, even at his feet, and that now she was studying, almost serenely, his penis resting heavily on his closed thighs.

She looked away.

And it was not, she realized in the next moment, the first time she had had to look away, cringing within herself at what had preoccupied her.

"My God," she muttered, "will you *please* learn to wear clothes!"

She viciously pulled the dresser drawer open and withdrew the torn pair of pants; she had, inexpertly, fashioned them from a pair that Paul claimed he no longer needed. "When I fix these," she said, the words clipped, harsh, "you *will* wear them." She threw the pants back into the drawer, slammed it shut, and hurriedly left the room. She locked the door behind her.

It was too late, Lumas realized. If Paul and Rachel were going to be told, if they were going to be warned— and, Christ! they had to be warned—they'd have to come to him. But that was something neither of them would do. Not in time, at least. Not before nightfall. After that, they could question him all they wanted, but there'd be no answers.

Answers? He'd never, he realized suddenly, really had any answers. He only knew *what* happened here, not why it happened, or how. Only *what*. And that was damned little to know. And damned little to die for.

I am a dying man, he thought. *And dying men are scared men. They tell themselves that the life they just finished living wasn't worth shit. Maybe they think it'll get them another chance.*

He grinned, his teeth jutting out starkly from behind dehydrated lips. It was a good thought—that dying men wanted another chance at life, that maybe they should have another try at what they tried for the first time around and missed—perfection.

Maybe in the last breath of the dying man there's a plea that someone close-by whisper, "You did your best. You did pretty good. It's all right." Maybe that last second of reassurance counts more than all the reassurance a man gets his entire life.

But, he reasoned, there were worse ways he could have spent his life than protecting what happened here; he could have been a merchant, like his father, and, like his father, care only about the money jingling in his pockets. *That* was damned little to die for—for the money they took out of your pockets, anyway, before they buried you, money that, by itself, probably made living more bearable but had no effect at all when it came time to die. You could cover a dying man with his money, you could stuff it in his mouth, and it would smother him. He'd choke on it. At least a poor and dying man had air to breathe.

He cursed, lifted his hands, suddenly, and held them close to his face: Just a bit longer, just a few seconds longer, and the boy would have joined those other two—"Joseph" and "Margaret." How merciful that would have been. But now the process would be agonizingly slow. Now it was a matter of waiting, and watching, and hoping. Though there was no hope.

Goddamn the little bastard! Why hadn't he shown himself sooner, when there was help for him. And guidance. He could have stolen from the traps all he wanted (for it had been the boy, Lumas realized now, just as he had suspected), as long as he stayed in his place, as long as he forgot the resemblance between himself and the Griffins, as long as he remained what he was. And didn't corrupt what he was.

A tear formed in Lumas' eye. Slowly, though not painfully—because the pain had left him days before—he sat up on the bed, studied the strip of leather holding the door closed, and stood. He cocked his head first to the right, then to the left. Was that, he wondered, only the sound of rain filtering through the trees and onto the roof? He took several slow steps toward the door. And stopped. No, he told himself; the rain had never sounded like that. He smiled. It had happened, he realized. It had happened and they were waiting for him. How terribly hungry they must be. And how well they knew what was being offered them.

More quickly, he took the several steps remaining to the door, reached out, and took the strip of leather in his hand. He hesitated. What if they did as the boy had done? What if, after all these years, they ended their new lives in a matter of months? It was possible. And if they did, then it was better that their lives be ended now. This day.

He glanced at the old, never-used shotgun standing up in the corner. And knew that, even if he could lift it and load it and fire it, it would make no difference. Because, in a second, they would be beyond his sight and hearing. Or —which was more likely, because they had no knowledge of guns, were only able to sense impending danger—they would be upon him, tearing frantically at his flesh while he still breathed.

He closed his eyes briefly. "Forgive me," he whispered. And opened the door. And felt the moist, cool air of nightfall moving over his face and hands.

CHAPTER 13

The brittle, continuous noise of the alarm clock finally roused Rachel. "Paul?" she murmured, eyes half open, trying in vain to focus on the white wall. "Paul, shut that off, would you?" She took her arm from beneath the quilt and felt behind her, on Paul's side of the bed. "Paul?" She rolled over on her back, savored, for a moment, the remnants of a particularly pleasant but rapidly fading dream, and forced her eyes to open wide. She looked to her left and sighed: So, he was already up. He *had* been telling her for several days how much better he felt, that the pain in his ribs was no longer constant, but intermittent:

"I can breathe again," he had explained, grinning. "Maybe I can stop using that lousy Darvon, or whatever it is. Gets rid of the pain, but makes me crappy as hell to live with, doesn't it?"

"At times," she'd answered.

She became aware, again, of the grating noise of the alarm. "Damn thing!" she muttered, and, her movements made awkward by fatigue, she climbed out of the bed, fumbled with the clock a moment, then succeeded in shutting it off.

She shivered spontaneously and glanced down at herself. *How in the world* . . . She hadn't gone to bed like that, she remembered. It came to her—the frantic lovemaking. And the profound exhaustion that followed. She saw the trailing edges of her blue nightgown beneath the quilt at the foot of the bed. She smiled wistfully, gratefully. Perhaps, she considered, the experience with the child the previous evening had prompted their lovemaking. Good news sometimes had that effect. She fished the nightgown from beneath the quilt and slipped it on. *Good news?* Well, yes—hearing words from the child was certainly not bad news. Admittedly, the words had only been in imitation of words she had said to him over and over again; words chosen for their simplicity—he had probably not understood their meanings. And, admittedly, he'd only repeated the two simplest of those words—"cat," "dog"—but wasn't that the way everyone learned to talk? If the boy had been mute all his life because he'd never, or hardly ever, been exposed to language, then the progress she and Paul had made with him was close to remarkable.

And that laugh. Such a highly developed, genuine laugh. Not at all the screeching laugh of a child. It was an infectious laugh, which, Rachel thought, the laugh of a child that age rarely is.

All of it had to mean that he was responding to her, coming out of the awful shell he'd been in ever since they'd found him.

"Paul?" she called, hoping he was still in the house so she could discuss with him the events of the previous evening. "Paul?" she repeated. There was no response.

A name, she thought suddenly. The boy needed a name. For too long they had referred to him only as "the child" and "the boy." Probably because as withdrawn as he'd been, she considered, as totally lacking in personality, the idea of giving him a name had just not occurred. But now . . . now that he'd spoken his first words, laughed his first laugh—

She mentally reviewed a few names. He wasn't a "Frank" or a "Mike" or a "Jerry." "Paul, Jr." certainly wouldn't do. His name had to be something lilting, poetic, and yet masculine. She grinned. She had gone through this process, she remembered—the frustrating, happy process of choosing a name—only a few times; just recently with Mr. Higgins, and, years before, with a dog her father had bought her, and, several years before that, when she'd barely been out of diapers, with her family of homemade dolls—Lucy, Elizabeth, Granny, Marjorie. She forced herself to abandon the memory. It had been, she realized, the stuff her dream had been made of—the dream from which she had been jolted by the alarm clock; something about those dolls—in reality so crude, but in the dream so wonderfully lifelike—dancing, at first grim-faced, then smiling, around her. And she had watched, pleased, delighted, and finally in an almost sexual ecstasy.

The remnants of the dream dissipated. She turned her head and looked into the kitchen. "Paul?" she called again, more loudly.

"I'm here," he answered from the kitchen.

What, Rachel wondered, was it that she had read, for an instant, on his face? Disappointment?

"Good morning," she said, smiling cheerily.

He was seated at the table, cup of coffee in hand. "Morning," he grunted.

Rachel looked past him; a freshly brewed pot of coffee, steam rising from its spout, was on the stove, a pan of rapidly boiling water on the burner beside it, a box of oatmeal on the counter.

"Oh," Rachel began, trying to sound pleasantly surprised, "you started breakfast. Thank you. I still hate to build a fire in that damned stove; I always burn myself." She went over to the counter and opened the box of oatmeal. "I've been thinking, Paul; about the boy: I think we should give him a name. Just temporarily. You know, until he's"—she tried to think of the right phrase—"well enough that he can tell us his name."

Paul said nothing.

"You don't like that idea, Paul?" She got a measuring cup from the cupboard and poured some oatmeal into it. "If you don't, I'll understand. It was just an idea. I mean, it's not like he's our own child, is it? It's not like we've adopted him or something." She went over to the stove and slowly poured the cup of oatmeal into the pan of water. "It's just that it seems kind of immoral to give names to, you know, the cat, and to the car"—they called it "Bessie" —"and even to your tractor"—he called it "Brutus"—"and go on referring to that child as 'the boy.' " She glanced at her husband. "Paul, are you listening to me?"

Paul's back was turned; she saw him lower his head slightly. "Yes," he said, "I'm listening. It's a good idea. I suppose."

"But you're not enthusiastic about it—is that what you're saying?"

He shrugged his shoulders, mumbled, "I don't know," turned his head, and looked blankly at her. "Rachel, did you leave that door open?" He nodded at the back door. It was closed.

"Last night?" Rachel began. "No, not that I remember." She thought a moment. "Wait a minute," she continued, "maybe I did. Just after you went upstairs to check on the boy, I was in here cleaning things up and I heard something like someone was on the back steps, so I opened the door and looked out. I didn't see anyone." She paused.

"It was probably a raccoon," she continued. "I remember once that one came right up to the back door. I imagine you could tame a raccoon if you tried hard enough." A quick self-conscious smile flashed across her face. Paul's face remained expressionless. "Well, anyway, I probably didn't close the door tight enough and the wind blew it open." She paused briefly. "I don't understand; what's so important about it, Paul?"

He stood abruptly. "I'll show you," he said. He strode briskly to the back door and opened it. "When I got up," he explained, "it was wide open." He pointed at the screen door. "And this is what I found."

Rachel looked to where he was pointing. "I don't see anything, Paul."

"Well, come closer, for God's sake."

She hesitated, surprised by his tone, then set the pan of oatmeal to one side and did as he'd asked. "Okay," she said, trying too hard, and knowing it, to sound annoyed, "what did you find?"

"These," Paul told her. He ran his finger along a small area about four feet up the right hand side of the screen door's frame. "These marks. Look at them."

Rachel leaned over slightly and, feigning disinterest, studied the marks. She straightened. "Well, I'm sorry, Paul. He does that all over; you should see the sides of the couch. I've scolded him for it, but you can't scold a cat, can you? It doesn't—"

"Hold it," Paul cut in sharply. "You think the *cat* did this?"

"Of course. He scratches on everything."

Paul gestured at the marks. "Take a better look, Rachel."

Rachel studied the marks more closely. She straightened.

"Well?" Paul coaxed. "Do you understand now?"

"I don't know," she whispered. She fell quiet for a long moment. She looked, Paul thought, near the point of tears. Then, "There's probably some kind of explanation, Paul. There has to be."

"Yes," Paul told her softly, "there is." He paused meaningfully. "The boy wanted to get out, couldn't reach the latch, or couldn't work it—which, I'm afraid, seems more likely—and so he tried to chew through the door. That's the explanation, and I'm sorry."

"No reason to be sorry, Paul," Rachel said, straining to sound flippant, her voice trembling. "I don't know about you, but I . . ." She bit her lower lip as if to steady her voice. "I never kidded myself about his . . . progress. He's got a long way to go . . ." She moved quickly back to the stove, repositioned the pan on the burner, and stirred the oatmeal slowly, methodically. "He's got a long way to go . . ." She hesitated, back to Paul. "This has got lumps in it, Paul. I'll have to start over again. You know how you hate—"

Paul, still at the screen door, heard the muted crack of the wooden spoon being driven viciously into the bottom of the pan—once, then again, and again.

For a moment, there was silence.

"Rachel," he pleaded, "don't . . ." He stopped, confused; though Rachel's back was turned, he sensed that she was smiling. "Rachel?"

She turned her head; a grimly satisfied smile, as if some dark suspicion had suddenly been confirmed, a long and bitterly fought battle finally won. "Hank will know what to do," she said, her voice steady.

"Hank is dead, Rachel. There's no doubt of it. You know that."

Her smile faded slowly. She said nothing.

"Rachel?"

"He told you, Paul." A hoarse, desperate whisper. "He told you and you wouldn't listen."

"Told me what, Rachel?" He took a few steps toward her, stopped, and nodded at the severely pointed, broken handle of the spoon she held menacingly in front of her. "Rachel"—his tone solicitous—"what are you going to do with that?"

"What Hank started to do—what you stopped him from doing, Paul."

"What in the hell are you talking about?"

She turned toward the living room. Paul reached out and grabbed her wrist. "Rachel!"

More because of the abruptness of her movements than her strength, she wrenched free of his grasp. Seconds later, she had crossed through the kitchen, and the living room, and had thrown open the door leading to the stairway.

Paul, confused, reacted slowly. Running through the living room, he could hear her; she was near the top of the stairs, he estimated. He pulled the door open—Rachel had slammed it shut behind her. He caught a fleeting glimpse of her nightgown as she rounded the top of the stairs and started for the back of the second-floor hallway—toward the boy's room.

"Rachel, stop!"

He took the stairs three at a time. On the landing he paused an instant, his wide-eyed and out-of-focus gaze on the bare wood floor, his hand clasped hard to his ribs. He took a deep breath and looked down the hallway. The boy's door, he saw, was open. Trying in vain to disregard the agonizing pain in his ribs, he stumbled down the hallway. "Rachel," he gasped, the word barely audible, even to himself, "don't!"

It was a grotesque and unbelievable scene that greeted him when he reached the boy's room. But, he knew, as grotesque and as unbelievable as it was, he was powerless, now to affect it.

"Rachel, darling . . ." A plea.

And before Paul fell to the floor, unconscious, the boy —prone on the cot at the far end of the room—looked over, and Rachel—arm upraised over him, the broken spoon held tightly in her hand—looked over. And the boy's face, as usual, but impossibly, was blank, and Rachel's face bore the same grim smile that had first appeared on it less than a minute before.

The world from which Paul struggled—first reluctantly, then with desperation—back to consciousness was a world of memory; memory that, once released, became uncontrollable because it had been denied for so long. A world inhabited by himself and his father and all the forms two such people can take:

Samuel Griffin, new father—his pride and happiness muted by the death of his wife in childbirth.

Paul Griffin, infant, waiting long hours alone at the farmhouse for his father to finish a day's work.

Samuel Griffin shutting the house up tight against a fierce winter storm.

Paul Griffin, miraculously averting death from pneumonia, cradled tightly in his father's arm.

Paul Griffin listening, barely comprehending, as his father speaks, in tones of deep respect, of "Lumas, my old friend."

Samuel Griffin—remembering his wife—weeping openly, unashamedly, but somehow no longer with sadness.

Father and son wandering the darkened forest, and the father's words: "Some will tell you, son, that the oceans are the source of all life." Then—with a slow, sweeping motion of his arm, a motion designed to encompass the forest—"but now, this is."

The whole thing both kaleidoscopic and a process of maturation. And Paul, an integral part of it—as observer and participant—more convinced of its reality than of the reality of Rachel wielding the broken spoon, of fields to be planted, of vandalized and restored farmhouses and the marks of human teeth on screen doors.

Reality so stark, so inescapable, that to finite understanding it became illusory.

And Paul fought to escape from it, its grip on him suffocatingly strong—each scene, as it swept past, a mere fraction of a second in length, was timeless, as if painted on a revolving wheel of immense size.

The last day, the day of his father's death, shimmered by.

Then the following day, a day of torturous silence, at first, as if the land beyond the farmhouse and the farmhouse itself had become separated from the flow and events and noise of existence. And then, with the approach of evening, a merciful silence. To Paul Griffin's young mind, trying to grope its way out of confusion and grief, existence had hushed itself temporarily as a show of respect to the man lying dead.

Then the silence was broken by the sound of someone walking very slowly up the stairs to the bedroom where Paul tried to sleep.

"Father," Paul said, "is that you?"

The footfalls grew heavier.

"Father?"

The noises stopped. Paul Griffin slept.

And was awakened by the knowledge that something was touching him very lightly, as a spider would, on the forehead, on the cheeks, on the arms.

And, barely discernible in the darkness, the face of a child—expressionless but, somehow, bearing curiosity, not question, and empathy, not sympathy, but bearing it as if in judgment of Paul's bewilderment and grief, as if finding out if the emotions gave pleasure or pain.

And the wheel had completed its revolution, had once again come to the beginning, the death of Elizabeth Griffin, the birth of her son, Paul, the long hours alone at the farmhouse, shutting the house up tight against the winter storm, Samuel Griffin weeping openly, unashamedly, but not with sadness.

Paul Griffin fought to make himself more an observer than a participant, fought to question—as he hadn't then—his father's words: "Some will tell you, son, that the oceans are the source of all life. But now, this is." Words so very difficult to comprehend, then, words so damnedly difficult to accept now.

"No, Father," Paul said aloud. "You're wrong. You have to be."

"Paul? Please answer me, Paul."

"The only things created here, Father, are the crops we grow, the wood we use as fuel and to build our houses . . ."

But there was no answer from Samuel Griffin. He lay dead in the far field while his young son waited, grief-stricken and confused, in the second-floor bedroom—waited for the dark expressionless child to speak.

And it was once again the time of death and the time of birth.

"Paul, please, please answer me!"

"Rachel?"

"Some will tell you, son, that the oceans are the source of all life. But now, this is."

"I don't know what you mean, Father. Tell me what you mean."

"Paul?"

"Rachel?"

"Please answer me, Paul."

"Tell me what you mean, Father. Tell me what you mean. Father? Father?"

The immense wheel slowly receded.

Finally, mercifully, it was Rachel whose face was before him, and it was not expressionless; it bore, intermittently, confusion, anger, anxiety.

"Rachel . . . the child . . ."

"He's all right, darling."

"You didn't—"

"No." She averted her eyes briefly. "No. He's all right."

Paul attempted to maneuver himself into a sitting position on the hallway floor. The pain in his side stopped him. "Goddammit!" he murmured.

"Is it your ribs, Paul?"

He nodded slightly.

"Do you think you can get down the stairs?"

"I don't know. Not right now."

"I can help you, Paul."

He tried to smile, but his lips only quivered.

"I *can*, Paul."

"Just . . . let me lie here another minute. I'll be okay."

Rachel said nothing for a moment. Then, "About the child, Paul." She waited for him to signal her to continue. He said nothing. "About what I was going to do. It was . . . like before. When we first found him. Do you remember?"

"Remember what?"

"What I said then, about knowing . . . about knowing and not knowing. Do you remember?"

"Yes, I remember." And despite his pain, the remark was patronizing in tone.

"It happened again, Paul. When I saw . . . when you showed me what you'd found. It happened again. Just like before. And I couldn't help myself."

Paul slowly raised himself up on his elbows, right hand pressed firmly to his ribs, gaze on the dark wall. "Why, Rachel?"

"I don't know," she answered flatly.

Paul closed his eyes momentarily—a silent refusal to accept her words. "Help me up, would you?"

With effort, and with Rachel's arms under his, he stood.

CHAPTER 14

When she thought about it, and there was rarely a time that she didn't, Rachel found herself more angry, confused, and (looking inward) frightened than ashamed by what she'd done. The only shame she felt was because of her *lack* of shame. The only comfort for her, she knew, was in the fact that, at the last moment, mercy or cowardice—she wasn't sure—had stopped her.

Paul, she realized, did not and could not understand. It was far too much to ask of him. Because *she* did not understand. The harshly illuminated, but only briefly glimpsed, truth had darkened once again.

Paul hadn't used the words *I don't understand.* If he had, he would have been asking for an explanation, a reason. And the explanation he'd accepted, had been forced by his love for her to accept, was embodied in the three words she'd used: "I don't know." Words at least vague enough, or ambiguous enough, that he didn't have to center on them, because they were externalizing words—they put the explanation outside her, beyond the scope of her responsibility. And that, in the face of her act, was a comforting thing.

He had watched her. Although his ribs had stopped giving him pain several days after his collapse in the second-floor hallway, and there was much work left to do in the fields, he had found one blatantly false excuse after another to stay in the house with her, or near it.

Until today. Three weeks after her attempt on the child.

"You think you'll be all right alone here for a few hours, Rachel?" He had finished his breakfast, was carrying his plate and silverware to the sink.

The words *Do you trust me?* nearly slipped off her tongue; instead, she said, "I think so. Why?"

"I've got something to do." He set his plate gently into the sink.

"Something to do?"

"Yes. It's been bothering me—"

"Mr. Lumas?"

"How'd you know?"

"I knew."

"Uh-huh." He paused, thought. His back was turned. "It's not something I want to do, Rae. I wish to hell somebody else could do it. But there is no one else, is there?"

She said nothing; there was, they both knew, a whole townful of people only ten miles away.

"So . . ."

"You think he's dead, don't you, Paul?"

"You don't?"

"We've said he is."

"And?"

"And I suppose we believe it. I suppose we have to."

"For our own peace of mind, you mean?"

"Yes. That's what I mean."

"Forget it, Rachel. There are more important things."

"I know it. There's no need to remind me."

A momentary silence. "Yes," he said. "You're right. I'm sorry."

She said nothing.

"Anyway," he began, "I won't be bringing him back, if it bothers you."

"Jesus, Paul!"

"I'll . . . I'll be burying him out there. I think he'd like that. Don't you think he'd like that?"

Confused silence.

"No one will know except us, darling. He had no family—he told me that. If we were to report his death, well, it would, you know . . ." He trailed off.

"Yes?" Rachel said.

"It would complicate things. Don't you think it would complicate things?"

"Yes. I do."

"Well then . . ."

"I'll be all right here. Don't worry."

"You're sure?"

"I'm sure."

He had been gone not quite a half hour; unless he walked very slowly—put it off in that way—he was probably at Lumas' cabin by now, had found the man's body, might even be scouting around for a proper burial site. Close to the cabin would be good. Of course, as with the two children—Margaret and Joseph Schmidt—there would be no coffin, only, perhaps, a blanket or a sheet . . .

Rachel shook her head briskly, as if to shake the thought away (how easily they had slipped out of what had become, what was, their previous life. As if they had been unplugged from it. And the kind of light that life had given them was gone, no longer made any real sense).

She shifted the tray she carried so it balanced on her right arm and pulled the stairway door open with her left hand. She cursed. Why in hell hadn't Paul put a bulb in the stairway, as she'd asked him to do so many times? A ten-minute job, that's all. It was dangerous the way it was. She remembered the last time—her foot, on the landing, reaching and readying itself for another step, and there wasn't one.

But, cautious, she ascended the stairs without incident, and moved, still cautious, down the darkened hallway toward the boy's room. At his door, she again balanced the tray on one arm, fished the skeleton key from her pants pocket, and opened the door.

The boy's light was on, though it did little more than alter the darkness slightly.

"Hello," she said.

"Hello," the boy said, his voice, as always, disconcertingly close to hers.

He was at the window, his back to her. And he was naked.

"Are you hungry?" Rachel said.

"Hello," he said.

Perhaps, Rachel thought, studying him, it was the light, or that her eyes were adjusting to it, or had overadjusted and would soon be returning to normal.

"Are you all right?" she said.

"Hello," he said.

Or maybe it was a combination of the feeble artificial light and the sunlight coming in through the boarded-up window.

"Did you sleep?"

"Sleep," he said.

It was his color, she thought. It had faded, or it appeared to have faded.

"I'm sorry," she said. It was a spontaneous phrase, a phrase she had used often since her attempt on his life. But, she knew, it encompassed much more than that.

"Are you all right?" she repeated.

"Hello," he said.

She set the tray of food on top of the dresser, took a few steps toward him. *Damn, if only the light was better.*

"I've brought you your breakfast. Are you hungry?"

"Sorry," he said.

She pursed her lips. She could, as she had a dozen times, go on like this with him for hours, hoping that, finally, he would make a sensible reply. But not *this* morning.

She felt in back of her for the doorknob, found it, and pulled the door open an inch. There was much to do. Because the child had repeatedly torn off the various articles of clothing she'd made for him, she had devised what Paul grimly referred to as "the straitjacket"—a one-piece green corduroy suit which, when finished, would fit snugly around the boy's neck, terminate at his thighs, and lace securely down his back. Paul and Rachel had agreed that he'd have to be a contortionist to get out of it. It smacked of cruelty, Rachel thought, but if the child did not soon learn to wear clothes, at least before autumn set in, he might fall victim to the same fatal illness Margaret Schmidt had succumbed to . . . She wondered, suddenly, why the poor, dead girl had occurred to her. What did she have in common with this young boy?

She pulled the door open wide, turned. From below, she heard the back door being pushed open. "Paul?" she called. She almost added, *Is Hank all right?* but realized it would be a foolish question. "Paul? Is it done?" Silence.

She locked the door behind her and walked quickly down the hallway to the top of the stairs.

She stopped and looked confusedly at the closed door at the bottom of the stairway. Had she closed it when she'd gone up to the boy's room? She wondered.

"Paul?" she called again.

There was no reply.

Greased paper normally covered the one east-facing window of Henry Lumas' cabin. The paper had been torn from the frame and, through an opening between the pines beyond, the morning sunlight sharply exposed to Paul what lay on Lumas' bed. The rest of the room was in near darkness.

Very slowly and quietly, as if not to disturb the room and what it contained, Paul pushed the cabin door shut.

"Hank?" he said. And cursed himself. It was all too clear that what lay on the bed was not the man he'd come to bury, that Henry Lumas was far beyond the pathetic and essentially empty gesture of burial. For, Paul thought, you do not bury a man's clothes. You don't say comforting things over a man's clothes.

He cursed himself once more and took a few halting steps forward.

Lumas' red-flannel shirt had been shredded viciously, only the arms remained more or less intact. His faded brown pants had been torn in half down the crotch and down the back; the two halves lay crumpled at the foot of the bed. There were smatterings of blood on the remains of the shirt, but nowhere else, except at random on the floor around the bed. It was apparent that, mercifully, Lumas had been attacked long after he'd died. If not, Paul reasoned, the room would have been awash with his blood.

Several emotions swept over Paul: Confusion; what animal would, or could, go to the trouble of removing Lumas' clothes before making a meal of him? Fear; not because of the scene itself—it was frightening only by extension—but because of the knowledge that whatever had attacked Lumas was doubtless still lurking somewhere in the forest. Grief; though muted by the circumstances of Lumas' death. Despite his apparently senseless attack on the child—made only a little less senseless by what Rachel had done; that apparent and silent conspiracy spoke only softly of sense or reason, and shouted of hysteria—Lumas had been a good, kind, and sensitive man, in many respects much like Paul's father. And when such a man dies, there is good reason for grief.

Paul buried his face in his hands and closed his eyes tightly, as if to strengthen the grief he felt. A tear moistened his fingers, then another. And he realized that the tears were not for Lumas, but for himself, and for Rachel. Tears caused by the confusion, the agony that life here had become. Tears that now flowed freely through his fingers, down the back of his hands, and onto the crude, dark floor. "Hank," he murmured. "Hank, goddamn you!" It was a curse of necessity. Something had to be cursed.

He let his hands fall. For a second, he flirted with the idea of burning the cabin to the ground, as if that would erase all that had happened in the past several months—erase it or cleanse it. But it was a foolish thought, and he knew it.

He turned and looked up at the cabin's severely peaked ceiling. Were those small sounds the sounds of rain? he wondered. But that was impossible. All morning the sky had been pale, quiet, and cloudless, without a hint of rain. Too beautiful a day to perform the grim task he had supposed had to be performed.

Rachel put her hand against the wall to steady herself on the stairway. "Paul?" she whispered. "Is that you?"

There was no reply.

"Paul, if you're down there, please answer me."

The closed door at the bottom of the stairway rattled a little on its hinges.

"Paul, please!" Still at a whisper, but taut, desperate.

And a voice from the other side of the door said, "Paul?"

Rachel stopped. The voice, she realized, had been her voice—made slightly hollow, just a bit off-key by the closed door. It repeated itself, "Paul?" And added, "Is that you?"

The long sliver of dull light along the bottom of the door, Rachel saw, was cut at the left and at the right by shadow.

"Paul?" she pleaded aloud, and tremblingly, "don't play games with me, Paul." But Paul didn't play such games, did he? Paul *couldn't* play such games. He was too somber for such games. Especially now. Today.

"Paul?" she said. And, on tiptoes, she descended the last few steps. She put her ear to the door, her hand lightly on the knob. "Paul, please answer me," she said. She tightened her grip on the knob. Turned it. And hesitated. "Paul?" she said.

"Paul, don't. Please answer me, Paul."

An echo, she told herself. *A kind of echo.*

"Don't," repeated the voice on the other side of the door. "Please answer me, Paul." And added, "Paul?"

Suddenly, Rachel pushed on the door. It did not respond. "Oh, my God!" she muttered. She pushed harder. And in vain. "Oh, please," she wept, relaxing her grip on the knob and lowering herself to a knees-jutting, head-forward sitting position on the stairs, "whoever you are, please, please go away."

"Please go. Oh, my God!" said the voice at the other side of the door.

It couldn't be rain, Paul told himself, And yet, of course, he amended, it was. Some changes took place very quickly here, the weather especially. It had to be a very light rain, it was barely audible, like mice running about on the roof. And, as well, sunlight still illuminated Lumas' bed, Lumas' shirt and pants—what was left of them. And what was left of them, Paul mused, was—along with the small, grimy cabin—probably all that was left of Lumas, the man. He caught himself on the qualifier. Had he been too quick to assume that whatever had attacked Lumas had been successful in dragging him off? Perhaps Lumas—an unusually strong man—had been able to defend himself, had driven the animal away, and then, in panic, fled the cabin. It was possible, Paul concluded, but not probable. Lumas was simply not the type to panic. And the evidence of his shredded, barely bloodstained clothes was damning evidence indeed.

Paul strode quickly, mechanically, to the bed, hesitated an instant, scooped the shredded shirt and pants into his arms, turned, and started for the door. He stopped, his gaze on the shotgun standing up in the southeast corner of the room. Lumas, he remembered, had once shown him the weapon, had, in fact, waxed enthusiastic about it. "I don't use it," he'd said. "Never needed to. Probably never would. But it sure is one hell of a fine gun, don't you think?" Paul had only smiled and nodded. Now, darkly aware that what had happened to Lumas could easily happen to him, and cursing himself for not having had the sense to have brought his own rifle, he took the shotgun from its place against the wall, studied it briefly, dispassionately—as if it had become some necessary but uninteresting extension of his arm—and made for the door.

He stopped once more. The rain was letting up, he realized.

The sliver of light along the bottom of the door, Rachel saw, had suddenly become whole again.

"Paul?" she murmured. Dimly, she was aware of how useless it was to call to him. It was not Paul at the other side of the door. He was still at Lumas' cabin, or had, by now, involved himself in the grim process of burying what remained of the man. Even so, the possibility for communication existed. It always existed.

"Paul?" she repeated.

From somewhere in the living room, but not from in front of the door, she heard Paul's voice. "I love you, darling," it said.

Then her own voice, but not her voice; "Oh, Paul," it said. "Oh, Paul."

She screamed—a high, shrill, piercing, abrupt scream —and pressed her hands firmly to her ears. She heard, through her hands, the scream repeated.

"Oh, Paul," she wept, "We must leave." And for one beautiful, impossible moment, she was back in New York, back in her small hot apartment. And she could hear, through the wall, that her neighbors—a middle-aged couple —were having an argument; she could make out none of the words, but knew it was a horrible argument. It always was. They hated one another, loved one another, were inseparable.

Outside, a wailing ambulance was on its way to somebody's misfortune.

It was early June. Paul Griffin had, the previous evening, asked her to be his wife: "I want you to be my wife,

Rae. Will you be my wife?" he'd said, and it was obvious that he felt foolish asking her that way.

"I'd like that," she'd answered, smiling gratefully, in spite of herself.

And now, listening to the drone of her middle-aged neighbors, she laughed.

The moment ended.

She became aware of a presence at the top of the stairs. She turned her head only slightly. It was the boy.

"What . . . what . . ." she stammered.

The boy laughed—that mature, infectious laugh so terribly unlike the laugh of a child, so terribly unlike what the laugh of a child could possibly be.

And Rachel laughed again a cold, hysterical laugh, and heard that whatever was at the other side of the door was laughing with her.

CHAPTER 15

Paul knew it and tried, hard, to cope with it. But it was impossible. It's possible, he reasoned, to cope with only what is familiar, what is recognizable. Coping with something that did not show itself, that remained hellishly anonymous, is not possible. You don't cope with ghosts; you experience them.

He knew it; there was no wolf. The last wolf had been killed seventy, eighty years before, as he'd told Rachel. Wolves left tracks. He had seen none. Wolves howled from time to time. But the only sounds here were the sounds one expected, sounds that were at least vaguely identifiable. Wolves, as well, had their own way of killing, and though it was terribly effective, it was also a messy way of killing. Messier than had been evidenced by the poor ravaged animals he'd found.

There was no wolf. But something else.

Suddenly, he remembered his final conversation with Lumas. He hesitated to think of it as a "coherent" conversation, or, for that matter, as a conversation at all, but more a monologue. A monologue Lumas felt *had* to be delivered before death claimed him. A kind of perverse last will and testament:

"The land . . ." Lumas had stammered. "The land . . ." he'd repeated, obviously reaching deep within himself for the correct words. "The land, Paul. The land creates."

Everything the man had said had revolved about that statement, Paul remembered. But none of what he'd said had been any more explicit, any less vague. Quite obviously, Paul reflected, Lumas had been employing his own opaque brand of subtlety. His references to Rachel's "gifts" had been especially opaque. If she possessed any gift, it was the questionable gift of an acute sensitivity coupled, damnedly, with a remarkable imagination. Evidence the voices she claimed to have heard from behind the closed door two weeks earlier. Evidence, also, the occasional and barely audible laughter she claimed to hear, on certain nights. Laughter that seemed to originate, she said, from somewhere within the forest. Laughter that Paul had not heard, though his hearing, he'd reminded her, was excellent.

And so, his deception, or half-truth: that he was going out, each day, in search of "the wolf." A deception for her sake. She could picture a wolf. She could mentally hold on to it. As he could. But the ghosts that actually inhabited the land were something else entirely. No, he amended, they were—as far as his knowledge of them was concerned— even less substantial than ghosts. They were . . . a vacuum. Something impossible for him to hold on to. And if Rachel tried to deal with it, it would tear her apart from the inside.

And so his deception, for Rachel's sake—wonderful, sensitive, vulnerable Rachel—would continue until he'd found whatever he was looking for. Or until it found him.

These thoughts preoccupied Paul for more than half the distance down the path to the forest. He stopped short, the rifle came to rest at a horizontal position in his hand.

He glanced critically at it. He had had little experience with rifles. He knew only that their primary function was to kill, and that made them obscene. He knew also that obscenity was necessary, on occasion. What had been done to Henry Lumas, for instance, was an obscenity. Not the instinctive actions of an animal satisfying its hunger. An obscenity. It required the obscenity of a rifle bullet to answer it.

He glanced in back of him, up the path toward the house, certain that his preoccupation with Rachel and with Lumas had caused him to overlook something. But the path was empty—the brightly sunlit trees and bushes to either side were curiously motionless.

He closed his eyes briefly, as if that temporary loss of sight would make his other senses more acute. He heard nothing. Felt nothing. Only stillness.

And it struck him that the stillness was not the ordinary stillness of midafternoon—that there was no busy undertone of foraging honeybees, birds involved in mating and food-gathering, small animals slipping through the underbrush. Sounds he had grown so accustomed to they had become a part of silence. The stillness he sensed was complete, as if all that existed around him was only some vast, circular, and wonderfully executed painting of what had once existed, an exhibit: *This has passed. This is history. Turn the page.*

He thought of cupping his hand to his mouth and shouting, "Hello, hello," but felt that, strangely, it would be an oafish thing to do, a cowardly thing to do. He could not admit that it would also be proof of the sudden, strong fear that had settled over him. That if the land and all that existed on it had gone into a sleep, his shouts would awaken it. And awaken the ghosts. Give them notice of his presence and his apprehension.

From the doorway, Rachel quietly watched the boy for a long moment. His back was to her, his face pressed hard against the boarded-up window. She could dimly see the contours of his tensed muscles beneath the green corduroy suit. Amazingly, the first time she had dressed him in it, several days before, he made no attempt to get out of it.

"Care to tell me," she said, realizing and relishing her facetiousness, "what it is you see out there?" She paused. The boy gave no indication that he knew she was in the room. "Is it freedom?" she continued. "Is it freedom you see?" She found that her tone had become vaguely pitying. "We all lose our freedom," she went on. "We have to. I lost mine to Paul. He lost his to this house. And you lost yours to us. That's the way it has to be. I'm sorry, but that's the way it has to be."

The boy did not move.

Rachel took a few steps into the room. "It's the sunlight you want, isn't it?" she said. "And I'll admit that we're being terribly unfair—keeping you cooped up in this dreary room. But it's the prerogative of parents to be unfair, isn't it?" She took another step toward him. Still he gave no hint that he knew she was in the room. "It's for your own good. I want you to know that. If we were to let you outside, as if you were a normal child, you might go back. And we don't want that."

She heard the sound of cloth being torn, seams pulling away from seams. The sounds stopped abruptly.

She stepped forward and studied the boy more closely. "What are you doing?" she whispered. He was in precisely the same position he'd been in when she'd entered the room. "Don't do that," she ordered, unsure of what it was she didn't want him to do. "What are you doing?" she repeated, because she heard again the sound of cloth being ripped, seams parting.

Then, impossibly, the boy's flesh—from his waist to under his right arm—appeared beneath the torn corduroy suit.

Rachel gasped. "What are you doing?" she screamed.

She ran to him, bent over, and spun him around viciously. He faced her eye to eye, expressionlessly, for only a second, then closed his eyes, as if in meditation, and tensed his muscles powerfully.

The left hand seam burst.

Before realizing what she was doing, Rachel allowed her open hand to sweep hard across his face.

The seams on the legs of the corduroy suit burst simultaneously.

"My God," Rachel murmured.

She raised her hand to strike him again. And hesitated. For the first time, she saw, an emotion was clear on his face. An emotion that, like his laughter, was a contradiction, an abomination. And, she realized in the next moment—as the shreds of the corduroy suit fell to the floor around him —that she was the source and the target of his emotion.

This is how the deaf must experience the world, Paul told himself. The thought was inaccurate, he knew. The world of the deaf was the same world he normally inhabited, and that world was filled with motion. This world was not.

The thought—offhanded, desperate, inaccurate—had been designed to give him comfort, he realized, had been designed to make him an observer. Not a participant.

He mentally cursed the logic of that conclusion.

He was, he knew, both observer and participant. But, he asked himself, of what?

Was this only some sacred pause in the progress of things?

"Hello," he shouted.

He shuddered violently: The word had been absorbed by the land in much the way it would have been absorbed by a small and cluttered room. As if the vastness around him was only an illusion.

Then the word came back to him from the forest—a quarter mile distant—and he smiled, relieved.

"Hello," he shouted again.

"Hello," he heard a second later.

His smile broadened.

Far to his right, a hawk circled expectantly.

Ahead, close to the forest, a woodchuck waddled lazily across the path.

From a shallow weed-choked ditch behind him, he heard a flurry of activity; a moment later, a pheasant—several of its feathers trailing to earth behind it—took flight.

And, abruptly, all the nearly subliminal noises of the land returned.

In the same instant, Paul's face went blank. He brought his rifle to a ready position—diagonally across his chest, right hand on its stock, left hand on its barrel:

You there! he wanted to yell. But the words went unuttered.

Fear stopped them.

And confusion.

And knowledge.

CHAPTER 16

Rachel thought; he died in his sleep. During the night, anyway (while she and Paul were asleep).

She wanted to step into the room. It seemed so ludicrous that she couldn't; she had, after all, been with him most of the night. But now, less than a minute after summoning Paul—"It's the boy. I don't know—there's something wrong. I don't think he's breathing, Paul"—she could only wait in the doorway, arms at her sides, body erect, face blank in anticipation.

Is he dead, Paul? She wanted desperately to ask it, to have the final word said. Paul was taking so long, and this death was so grotesquely obvious. So without question.

Paul took his finger from the boy's jugular but did not straighten; he had his left knee on the floor, was resting his right arm on the other knee. "He's gone, Rachel."

"He's dead?" As if asking, *He's asleep? Has he eaten? Is he feeling better today?*

"Yes. He's dead."

"How, Paul?" *How do you change a tire, clip a cat's nails, use an ax?*

Paul stood very slowly, gaze on the boy all the while. "He's dead, Rachel—that's all I can say. If you want to know how, you'll have to ask someone else." He said it matter-of-factly, as if commenting on a not-quite-up-to-par meal; it gave the words a grim, cold finality.

"Was it me, Paul?"

He turned his head, looked confusedly at her. "You?"

"This room," she explained, face still blank, body still erect. "Did we kill him, Paul? Did we kill him by putting him in here?"

Paul turned back to the boy. "He died." Again matter-of-factly. "He's dead, that's all I can say, Rachel. And any . . . speculation as to how he died, or why, is going to be self-defeating."

"Jesus, Paul!"

"It's true, Rachel. And you should realize it."

She said nothing.

Moments later—when he turned away from the boy —she was gone. He listened, heard her go down the stairs, hesitate a moment, then cross through the living room and kitchen. Another hesitation. Then the back door and the screen door were opened; both doors shut seconds later.

Some things—weddings, for instance, and bad love-making—Rachel mused, are permanently fixed in the memory, and they're unalterable. All the pathetic, futile attempts made to stop a death are unalterable, too. A person might wish, afterward, that those attempts had been more in earnest, had put the death off a few hours or a few days. But the result would be exactly the same, wouldn't it?

She descended the back steps slowly, almost instinctively with caution. My God, it was a gorgeous day; brisk and clear and it had a good clean smell to it—the smell of autumn.

Permanently fixed; covering that exquisite brown

body with several blankets (warmth always put death off), even though she knew that, within minutes, he'd throw them to the floor. Smearing first-aid cream over those ugly dark splotches on his arms and legs. Forcing bouillon and mushroom soup and mashed peas into his mouth (hunger was a friend of death). Staying in that awful room with him for hours and hours, as if death couldn't happen unless she looked away. But it had, although the exact moment had escaped her notice. She might, she knew, have been watching him a long, long time . . .

Permanently fixed—all that she should have done to save him. She could, for one, have taken him into town where there would have been better help for him, although not as much caring (caring staved death off, too). And, during the first stages of his illness, letting him out of the house and into the healing sunlight. But she hadn't done those things, and never would—not even in memory. Instead, she had done the things which had killed him.

Goddammit! Did Paul listen, really listen, to some of the things that had come spilling from his mouth? "He's dead, that's all I can say, Rachel. And any speculation as to how he died, or why, is going to be self-defeating." Oh, that was very nice, very *rational*. And inhuman. You could expect some killing machine to feel nothing for what it did, but as for the person who operated the machine . . .

She stopped abruptly on the last step, her hand lightly touching the new railing.

She was, she realized, thinking objectively, logically. As Paul apparently had been. But it was impossible. Death precluded it. Especially this kind of death.

It was, she thought, as if something had been misplaced. It was not a sense of emptiness she felt, but merely that she had expected something and it had not arrived.

She grasped the railing tightly.

That something, she knew at last, was grief. Guilt,

131

yes. She had that in abundance—though it was not the self-defeating, self-destructive guilt Paul supposed it to be. It was far weaker, far more rational—dammit—than that. But no grief. Not for the boy. And not even for herself that she was now without him. It was as if a visitor had come and stayed and interrupted their lives. And now was gone.

She sat on the third step, hand still on the railing.

Was she . . . grateful? But that was impossible, too. She had been, for all intents and purposes, the child's *mother* these past few months. And now she and Paul would have to bury him, would have to dig a deep hole and put him in it and cover him because those arms, those legs, that chest, all of what just yesterday had been so wonderfully animated, would never again . . .

Oh, but she was being maudlin, wasn't she? Maudlin and dreary and . . .

But that was to be expected. Death made everyone maudlin. She grinned; at least she wasn't totally lacking in the correct responses.

"Rachel?"

She turned her head sharply. Paul was standing at the top of the steps. She half expected to see the boy's body in his arms.

"Paul . . ."

"Did I startle you?"

She grinned again, embarrassed. "Yes." She thought a moment. "What are we going to do with him, Paul?"

The question, she could see—or, she amended, the fact that she had asked it—confused him, She fought down a larger grin.

"*Do* with him?" Paul asked.

"Yes." She stood. "Are we going to take him into town? That would be the right thing, wouldn't it? Or are we going to bury him"—she turned her head briefly, nodded—"out there somewhere?"

"I don't know, Rachel." It was apparent by his tone that it was not, at the moment, what concerned him.

"Well, we've got to think about it, don't we, Paul?" It was more a statement than a question.

"Yes, of course. It's just that . . ."

"It's just that," Rachel cut in, "you don't understand my attitude. And I don't blame you. I don't understand it, either. If you'd prefer, I could go into shock . . ."

"Rachel, please."

"But I've read that the complete lack of emotion in cases like this can be a form of shock. So maybe I *am* in shock and don't know it. But I don't think so."

"Rachel, listen to yourself." He took a few steps toward her. "Do you know what you sound like?"

"I imagine I sound pretty awful. I'm sorry if I do. But facts are facts and we've got to face them. And the fact is—there's a body up in that room"—she nodded at the upstairs window; Paul took another step toward her —"and we've got to do something with it. Now, if we took it into town, we both know there'd be a lot of . . . uncomfortable questions, maybe even some accusations, and we don't want *that*, do we? No. At least *I* don't want it. I can't speak for you, and never would."

"Rachel, you're babbling."

"Babbling? No. Merely thinking out loud. And thoughts are sometimes less than coherent. Mine are, at any rate. Speech is, too. Lumas was quite often coherent. Do you remember?" She looked questioningly at Paul; he was within a few steps of her and moving very slowly.

"Yes," he said soothingly. "I remember."

"All that crap about *the land* and *creation*." She chuckled shortly, derisively. "If you ask me, Paul, he was

133

loony. Positively out of his gourd. Nutsed up. Insane. Though, on second thought, maybe he was just senile, as you said. Or maybe he had syphilis—did you ever think of that, Paul? It's possible. Don't you think it's possible?"

"It's possible." He was only a step above her now.

"And as for the boy, he was never incoherent. He didn't have the vocabulary for it. He was as coherent as . . . as that sky. Of course, you weren't with him very much so you didn't know him as well as I did. He was quite single-minded—"

In the weeks that followed, Rachel would reflect that it was probably Paul's touch—his hand gently on hers on the railing—that sparked her short-lived breakdown. She remembered none of her words—"Oh God, thank you, thank you." And, "It's over, isn't it, Paul?" were the most telling—and Paul, though she begged him for the details of her breakdown, refused.

CHAPTER 17

Nothing marked the spot—no crudely improvised cross, no stone. All Rachel knew, as she looked out their bedroom window, her hand holding the heavy curtain aside, was that the boy had been buried "north of the house." Although she had—uncertain why—asked Paul to show her the exact spot, he had reiterated "north of the house," and added, "That's all you need to know, darling. If you need to know even that." She was, she knew, grateful he had been so close-mouthed; if she had been with him at the burial and knew the spot, she would have made daily forays to it—perhaps to mutter, "I'm sorry," over and over again, as she had done before, or perhaps merely to remember and so regret. This way—"north of the house" —she could almost convince herself that the boy hadn't been buried at all, that, in fact, he hadn't even died, that when Paul had led her back into the house that morning— led her into the bedroom and told her to rest, "I'll do what's got to be done"—he had gone back upstairs and found the boy alive, miraculously revitalized, and had set him free. It was a comforting fantasy. A strong fantasy. Once, several days after the boy's death, she remembered, when she had recovered from her breakdown and the fantasy was just beginning to take hold, she had even imagined that she had seen him "north of the house"— his head, at least, though dimly because, as now, it was dusk. It—the illusion, the imagining—had first appeared at the periphery of her vision, and when she had turned her full gaze on it, it had held for a second—the dark face, the darker hair—then had vanished into the shoulder-high weeds.

She let the curtain fall: Someday, she vowed, she would tell Paul about that vision. Someday far into the future, maybe when they were very old and their entire experience with the boy could be looked upon as something that might or might not have happened: *Did it really happen, Rachel? I think it happened, but I'm not sure—it's hard to remember these days . . . I don't know, Paul. I wish there was someone we could ask about it.*

She smiled a self-pitying smile; it would never come to that, would it? Their memory of the boy would be a terrible burden on them for the rest of their lives. A terrible burden on her, at least. Paul seemed to think of the whole thing as an embarrassment, a kind of extended *faux pas*. But perhaps that was unfair, perhaps she wasn't reading him correctly. Perhaps there was vanity in the way she read him—a vanity that said he couldn't possibly feel the way she felt, couldn't possibly hold the overwhelming guilt she held. At first, in the first hours after the boy's death, it had been an easy guilt, a rational guilt. Then, almost overnight, it had become more than that, had been attended by the knowledge that she had caused the death of an exquisite and vibrantly alive creature. *That* was not rational, she knew; she had fed him well, had cleaned up after him, had shown him in many ways that she cared for him. Any other child would have . . . No, she amended, any other child would have survived it. And that was the key to her new guilt—*any other child.*

That special knowledge was always with her, but so elusive—like trying to remember a specific but rarely used word or a specific name because someone had asked. It would come spontaneously, but only seldom if an effort was made, and never if the effort was strong.

She turned her head. Paul was standing in the doorway, a vague look of admonishment on his face.

"What are you doing, Rachel?"

"Nothing," she said evenly. "Thinking, I guess."

"Rachel, we've got to talk. There's something . . ."

"And remembering."

"Punishing yourself, you mean."

She smiled again, again self-pityingly. "Yes," she whispered.

He sighed heavily. "We've got to talk."

His tone brought her up short, and she resented it, would have preferred to stay within herself a while longer. She said nothing; maybe he'd go away.

"There's something I haven't told you," he went on, his tone softer. He waited. Still she said nothing. "I don't know where to start." A pause. "Sit down, okay." He nodded at the bed, she didn't move from the window. The questioning look in her eyes said, *Go on. Continue. I don't want to sit down.* He closed his eyes briefly, sighed again. "I've thought about it, Rae. I've thought about it a lot in the last few weeks, ever since the boy . . . you know, ever since he died. And I think it's . . . I think . . . we've got to leave."

"Leave," she said, but not as a question or a statement, but as if it were a word she'd just learned and she was trying it out.

"There are . . ." He stopped, seemed uncertain how to continue. He looked questioningly at her, as if she might finish the sentence. She said nothing. "The day before the boy's death, I saw them, so I know. There are, I mean, others . . . like him, like the boy, Rachel."

He hadn't expected it—her short, brittle laugh; as if it were a physical blow it stopped his breathing for a moment.

"Are there, Paul? Are there *others?*" She laughed again.

"Yes," he managed.

"Yes, Paul? I thought you'd never notice, Paul."

"Rachel, please . . ." He had never before heard this shrieking sarcasm from her.

"Do you think I'm blind, Paul? Do you think you're the only one with any . . . any awareness, for Christ's sake? Do you think you're telling me something I don't know? Jesus, Paul, I've known it for months."

"No, I . . . I mean . . ." He gazed confusedly, helplessly, at her. "Yes," he continued, "I knew . . . I just . . ." His confusion and helplessness changed abruptly to anger. He said nothing more for a long moment, then turned and left the room.

Rachel's tears came when she heard the screen door slam shut, when Paul was safely beyond the range of her voice. "Oh, God," she murmured, "no. No!"

"One load," Paul explained. "We're not coming back."

They had acquired little in their stay at the house. If they had stayed another year or so, Rachel mused—transferring some of the clothes from her dresser drawers to a large, much-used suitcase—they would have had boxes and boxes of miscellaneous things: books, knick knacks, games, potted plants, all the et cetera that accumulates from being in one place, of calling a place home. But she hadn't been away from the house since the boy had come to them and Paul's trips to town had been primarily concerned with restocking their cupboards, so leaving the house involved, for the most part, repacking what they had unpacked just four months before.

Paul had made a few acquisitions: the rifle, three boxes of ammunition, and some paperback novels to augment the several dozen books they had brought with them. Having no TV or radio, Paul had proposed that when winter started settling in they could use some of their free time by reading to one another. It had been a romantic idea and Rachel had looked forward to it.

She closed the suitcase, locked it, and stood for a moment with her outstretched arms on it. They were wrong, she thought—all those who said a common enemy brought people together. It hadn't brought her and Paul together, it had put them in their own, private, confused, and self-protective worlds. Well, that was the operative word, wasn't it? *Confused.* If they had an enemy, they weren't certain what it was, or even that they could fight it. Perhaps they didn't share a common enemy after all, but shared uncertainty, shared confusion. If so, ending it this way, running from it, might bring them together once again. Perhaps that underscored Paul's decision to leave, and perhaps he wasn't even aware of it. She thought about that; it was a happy delusion, she concluded. She could cling to it if necessary.

She set the suitcase on the floor and replaced it with a brown vinyl two-suiter that had the look and smell of newness to it. Paul had bought it especially for their move to the house, she remembered.

The station wagon was not heavily loaded. "If you want," Paul said, setting a large box filled with dishes, pots, pans, and silverware on the tailgate, "we can find room for your desk and chair."

"No," Rachel answered, "that's all right." A pause. "Can we take the rug, though?"

Paul peered into the car a moment. "Yes," he said, "I think so." He straightened. "I'll get it in a second." He pushed the box forward, straightened again. "I'm sorry," he whispered, gaze on the house.

"No need, Paul. Let's not look backward, okay."

"Yes," he said tonelessly. He inhaled deeply, exhaled slowly. "I'll get that rug and we'll get going. We'll have to stop in town to close our bank account, you know, and settle things with Marsh and the glazier."

"Uh-huh." A pause. "I'll wait here while you get the rug, if you don't mind."

He stood quietly for a few seconds, then moved slowly down the shallow incline of weed-choked lawn to the house. When he'd closed the front door behind him, Rachel turned and critically examined his packing job. It was obvious he had done it hurriedly—the boxes and suitcases had not been packed into the car so much as thrown in randomly, and much of the available space had not been utilized. It didn't really matter, Rachel thought, but it wouldn't take long to tighten things up a little. She set to it.

Several minutes later, she remembered: "Damn," she muttered. They had forgotten the cat. Paul had probably conveniently forgotten it, she considered—he had never seemed to care much for the animal, had, more than once, even prepared to kick it when it had gotten in his way and his mood was bad.

On all fours, she backed out of the car's interior and stepped to the ground.

"Higgins," she called. "Mr. Higgins." She listened

for his answering meow from the thickets fifty feet south of the house. Nothing. "Higgins, here kitty-kitty." She waited. Still nothing.

She started down the lawn. Stopped. "Higgins, c'mere Higgins. Do you want to eat?" The cat had learned what the phrase meant and it never failed to bring him running. "Higgins!" She moved farther down the lawn, peered hard into the thickets. "*There* you are," she said, smiling as if the cat had been playing a game with her. He was just inside the shadows of a huge chokecherry bush, had obviously been sleeping there.

Rachel slapped her thigh. "Well, c'mon," she coaxed. "Do you want to eat?" The cat turned its head and blinked lazily at her. Sighing, she moved quickly across the side lawn and scooped him into her arms. "What'd you do, find a couple mice?" She stroked him; he purred loudly. "We're taking you to a new home, Higgs. You think you'll like that?"

She started back across the lawn. Stopped. Turned her head slowly. Out of the corner of her eye she had detected movement near the station wagon. "Paul?" she called, thinking it was him stowing the rug away.

"Yes?" he answered from within the house.

Rachel snapped her head to the left, then back toward the car. Because of the weeds and the slope of the lawn, she could see only its roof and the upper half of its windows.

A wisp of dust arose from behind the car and was followed almost immediately by a dull thumping sound. Rachel stared, confused. Another wisp of dust, another thump, then various metallic, tinkling sounds.

"Paul!" Rachel screamed. Cat in her arms, she ran up the lawn. A dozen feet from the car she halted, gasped spontaneously, heard Paul, behind her, vault across the porch, down the steps, across the lawn. "Rachel!" he called as he ran. "What's wrong, Rachel?" He stopped beside her. "Jesus Christ!" he hissed.

"I went looking for Mr. Higgins," Rachel explained unsteadily. "I thought I saw something . . ."

Here and there among the scattered boxes and suitcases—one of the boxes had popped open upon hitting the road, spilling its contents; books, clothing, an alarm clock, a toaster—Rachel and Paul both saw the footprints lightly traced in the earth to the side and in the back of the car and then to the opposite side of the road.

A child's footprints.

CHAPTER 18

Paul nodded at four, thin, parallel scratches, one seeping blood, on Rachel's left forearm. "Did you see those?" he asked.

Rachel gave the arm a cursory examination. "They're not deep," she told him.

"Well, maybe you should put something on them."

"No. It's okay. Let's go."

"It might get infected."

"I said it's all right, Paul." Her tone had sharpened. "He's scratched me before and nothing happened."

He attempted to reach out and touch the scratches; she jerked her arm away.

Paul put the car in gear. "We'll get something in town," he said tonelessly, and took his foot off the brake. The car rolled forward slowly; Paul was drawing this out, Rachel knew. He was saying good-bye to the house. Well, he was entitled . . .

"Paul, if you don't mind . . ."

He increased speed, though just slightly.

Against her better judgment Rachel craned her head around and stared blankly at the house.

"I'm sorry," Paul said.

"We didn't know," Rachel said, uncertain of the direction of his apology.

"We couldn't know. Not really."

The thickets that crowded up to the road hid all but the house's roof now. Rachel craned her head around farther to keep her eyes on it. Mr. Higgins climbed onto the back of the seat, then into her lap. She idly stroked the animal, her head turning slowly as the car took her farther from the house.

"Well, that's it," she whispered. She settled back, eyes now on the narrow road ahead.

"Yes," Paul said.

"That's it," she repeated, at a whisper.

"Yes." He took his foot off the accelerator to negotiate a long, slow curve. "Yes, that's it."

"Maybe it would have worked, Paul."

"Maybe."

"And maybe not."

"That's true."

"Well, it doesn't matter." God, this was worse than silence.

"No. It doesn't matter. Not anymore." He accelerated; the road was straight for another quarter mile.

"Do you think they were trying to keep us there, Paul? Throwing everything out of the car like that. Do you think it was a challenge or something." That was better. More to the point.

"It's possible." *It can wait, Rachel.* He cranked his window up against the road dust wafting into the car.

"Well, it's hard to say why they did it, isn't it? I mean . . . we don't know anything about them, do we, Paul?"

"No. Nothing." *Drop it, Rachel.*

"Why did they do what they did to the house, for instance?"

"We have no proof . . ."

"Who needs proof, for God's sake. Mr. Marsh didn't do it, and I'm certain Mr. Lumas didn't . . ."

"How can you be so certain of that?" Paul asked dryly. He brought the car nearly to a stop; a severe right-angle turn to the west confronted him. Out of the turn, he remembered, the road narrowed, and it would require all his attention to keep the car from wandering onto the soft shoulder to the left, or into the heavily wooded valley to the right. If—improbably—he met another car along that precarious half mile, one of them would have to . . .

"You don't really believe Lumas could have vandalized the house, do you, Paul?"

He was through the turn—the half mile was before him. He accelerated to just over ten miles an hour. "I really don't see that it matters a whole hell of a lot, Rachel. What's done is done, Lumas is dead—"

"Yes."

"And it's all behind us. As you said, let's not look backward. Those were the words you used."

"I know it. But we've got to . . . well, it's something that's going to be on our minds for a long, long time."

"Which means we don't have to talk about it now, do we?"

"You want me to shut up?"

"No . . . it's this damned road, that's all."

"I don't remember coming this way when we came up, Paul."

"Well, we did." He let off on the accelerator, the car's front right wheel lowered itself into a deep pothole, throwing Rachel against her door. The cat bounded from her lap and into the back of the car, its tail fluffed.

"Jesus," Paul muttered, touching the accelerator gently. He felt the back wheels spin for a second, catch on the loose dry gravel, and the car lurched forward. A second later, the right back wheel caught the pothole, throwing

Rachel toward the back of her door. She reached for her seat belt. "It's not you," she explained, hurriedly fastening the belt.

"It gets worse," Paul told her.

"I'm sure it does. All that rain during the summer."

"Uh-huh."

"You know, Paul, now that I think about it, the more convinced I am that it was a challenge."

"What?" Momentary confusion.

"Throwing our stuff on the road. They were challenging us."

Another pothole threw Rachel toward her husband, then violently to the right; the side of her head struck the window.

Paul glanced over at her. "You all right?"

Rachel rubbed her ear, attempted a smile. "Yes. Is it going to be like this all the way to town, Paul?"

He looked questioningly at her; she'd ridden this road before, surely she remembered. "Just a mile or so, then we'll hit Route 52."

"Oh yes. I remember now."

"And the road widens a couple hundred feet ahead."

"Uh-huh."

"We'll make it, Rae."

"I have no doubt . . . Paul?" A brief pause. "What are we running from?" She glanced at him, saw his grip on the wheel tighten, the suggestion of a grimace appear on his face. He said nothing.

"Paul?" She thought of repeating *What are we running from?* as if he hadn't heard her. "Why are we running?" she said and waited. "Paul?"

"We aren't running," he said flatly.

"Aren't we? What would you call it then?"

He chanced a quick look at her; she saw pleading in his eyes: *Later, Rachel, Later.* "I'd call it," he began, eyes

146

on the road again, "admitting that a situation has gone sour."

"Sour?"

"Bad. Unworkable."

"You were unhappy there—at the house?"

"Wasn't it obvious, Rachel?"

"That's not an answer."

"Yes, then. I was unhappy." A monotone.

"No, you weren't, Paul. Not with the house, not with what you were doing, only with the fact that the boy was with us. Even the others didn't matter that much."

"What are you driving at, Rachel?"

"Only that we've got to be honest about this; we aren't running from the house, or from what we'd planned, We're running . . . *Paul!*"

Paul braked hard, spontaneously; the car came to a quick halt, its backend dangerously close to the shoulder of the road.

"For God's sake, Rachel."

But she had thrown her door open and was stepping hurriedly out of the car.

"Rachel, what the hell?" He reached for her, but she was on the road now. She started toward the front of the car, stopped, her steady gaze fixed on something in the valley to the right.

Paul opened his door, stepped onto the road. "Rachel?" he said over the top of the car.

"Come here, Paul." He saw the upper part of her left arm move slightly, as if she was pointing.

"What is it, Rachel?"

"Come here, please."

Paul closed his door and moved around the front of the car. He stopped a few feet from Rachel and looked questioningly at her, though her gaze was still on something in the valley. She pointed again. He looked.

147

The body lay on its stomach in a small clearing a few yards up the valley's opposite slope, head turned to the right, legs splayed out, arms at its sides and turned inward, so the palms were up.

"It's one of them, isn't it, Paul?" Resignedly, desperately.

Paul said nothing for a moment, then, moving off the road and starting down the slope; "I'll get him. Wait here."

"Yes," Rachel said. "Be careful, Paul."

Nearly a half hour later, Paul, breathing heavily, laid the body gently on the road in front of the car. He straightened. "She hasn't been dead too long, Rachel. She's still warm."

Rachel leaned over the dark naked body, placed her hand on the girl's cheek. "She's beautiful, Paul." The word was accurate; as with the boy, Rachel knew, in life it would not have been. But now that death had settled over the girl's features, the word was no longer inadequate, no longer too restrictive.

"Yes," Paul whispered.

Rachel thought fleetingly, *They could have been twins, the boy and this girl.*

"Very much like the boy," Paul said, as if to himself.

"Yes," Rachel said. "That's what . . ."

"Well, we can't leave her here."

"Are you sure she's dead, Paul?"

Yes, I'm sure, his silence told her.

He bent over, slipped his arms behind the girl's knees and neck, straightened with the body in his arms. "Clear a place in the back of the car, Rachel."

"What are we . . . what are you going to do, Paul?"

"Bury her, of course."

"But maybe she's not . . . maybe she isn't one of them . . . I mean shouldn't we . . ."

148

"No. We shouldn't. Now, please do as I've asked. We're going back to the house."

"We can't do that, Paul."

"Just to bury her, Rachel. That's all."

"But why not right here?" She pointed tremblingly. "Down there where you found her."

"I have my reasons, Rachel. Trust me, please."

"I'll wait for you, Paul. I'll wait right here. Don't worry."

"You're coming with me. Now, clear a place in the back of the car."

It was clear from his tone that argument was useless. "They'll be waiting," Rachel said, and did as Paul had asked.

CHAPTER 19

It was only minutes before Rachel realized the truth, and not from anything Paul had said; if she had listened merely to his words, she would have believed he was doing what he said he was doing, and nothing more. But he was deceiving her. More than that, he had relegated her—no, she amended, had relegated her desperation to be away from the house—to a position of nonimportance; as if—in the thirty minutes it had taken him to go into the valley, take the girl's body into his arms, and, resting often, bring it back to the car—he had somehow been impressed with a great sense of duty, a nebulous but massive feeling of obligation, and her—Rachel's—presence while he performed that duty, met that obligation, was somehow necessary, while her protestations, her desperation, mattered not at all.

And so the truth hit her, though she couldn't pinpoint how, from what source: They were going back to the house. Paul was going to take them back. And they were going to stay.

She should not have gotten into the car with him, she thought suddenly. And, as suddenly, she rejected it. Even if, she knew, she had realized the truth sooner, it would have been impossible for her not to have gone back with him. And the reasons were simple: she loved him. Deeply. And she did trust him. It was herself she feared. Herself she could not trust. She did not fear the children. She feared her ignorance of them.

And yet, though she was able to categorize her fears, knew where they originated—an ability anathema to her ideas of herself—she *was* frightened. More frightened than she had ever been. More frightened, she thought, than one who knows death is imminent, but realizes its source. That fear, spawned by the quick, irreversible approach of death, is specific. Her fear, spawned not by what she knew, or thought she knew, but by the vacuum of not knowing, by the darkness of ignorance, could slowly, agonizingly, tear her apart. A self-torture she would be powerless to stop, or even control.

And she knew also that place, proximity, would exercise only a slowing action on that self-torture. New York, though it was hundreds of miles distant, though it was a wholly different world from the world she and Paul had planned to leave, would only temporarily salve or sublimate her fears. She could not run from an enemy which drew its identity and its intentions primarily from her imagination, from her need to fill the blank spaces. What had she said to Paul? *"They'll be waiting for us."* Her ignorance would have them waiting anywhere—at the house, in New York, in her dreams—lurking, waiting in the silence and darkness that would exist wherever she might be.

"Stop," she said, not as a command, or in desperation, but in resignation—a tone designed to tell Paul she knew what he was doing and she wanted to talk about it a moment without the distraction of the car lurching this way and that on the bad road.

"Why?" Paul said.

"Please. Just stop."

He glanced at her; she was not looking at him but at the cat lying in her lap—peacefully, now, after she had restrained it several times from leaping into the back of the car, curious about the girl's body.

"Rachel, we haven't got time."

"Please."

Sighing, Paul brought the car to a slow halt. He rested his forearms on the steering wheel, kept his eyes on the road. "Okay, what is it?"

She hesitated, unfocused gaze still on the cat; she was surprised to feel a tear slip down her cheek and onto the back of her hand. "I just want to know ... why, I suppose."

"Why what?" Apparent annoyance.

"Why we're going back. If you know."

He sighed again. "I told you why." He put his hand on the gearshift. She reached out suddenly, put her hand on his hand, looked pleadingly at him. "You owe them nothing, Paul."

"*Owe* them? What in hell are you talking about, Rachel?"

"I know what you're doing, Paul. I know."

The abrupt anger that tightened his features made her withdraw her hand quickly. "You don't know anything," he hissed. "You only think you do." He put the car in gear and floored the accelerator. The car's rear wheels spun a moment, then the left rear wheel caught on the loose gravel and the car fishtailed toward the center of the road. "Dammit," Paul whispered, letting off on the accelerator and pulling the wheel violently to the left; he lightly touched the accelerator, the car straightened, and they were moving again. A ten-minute drive remained.

Paul brought the car to a careful stop on the road in front of the house. Rachel, frowning, looked past him; *It hasn't changed*, she thought. It should have begun to disintegrate, evaporate, its walls and windows should have begun falling inward or outward as soon as they left it. She and Paul gave the house life, didn't they? It took something from them and existed because of them, so they were necessary to it.

"This is going to take some time, Rachel."

"Time?"

"A couple hours maybe. Why don't you wait in the house?" His slight smile was, she knew, designed to apologize for his anger of ten minutes before.

"Is that what you want, Paul? For me to wait in the house."

"Only a suggestion. I'm sure you wouldn't want to . . ."

"No. I wouldn't."

And the children weren't waiting. Of course. That had been a stupid, hysterical thing to say. And the house hadn't changed, hadn't metamorphized.

"Just a couple hours, maybe less," Paul said.

"Then we'll leave for good, Paul?"

"Yes." Comfortingly, reassuringly.

"I hope so, Paul."

He said nothing.

"I don't think I could stand it here another day, Paul."

He took a deep breath. "You underestimate yourself," he said on the exhale. And added, steadily, condemningly, "And sometimes you misjudge me." He opened his door and stepped out of the car.

Rachel ran her hand slowly along the top of the iron stove. She studied the hand. No dust. Not even that much in the way of change. It was all as they had left it.

Out of the corner of her eye she noticed the cat trotting from the living room toward the open front door. She crossed the kitchen quickly and closed the door. "No, Higgins," she said. The cat looked up at her, wide-eyed, and meowed once, pleadingly. "No," she repeated. The cat turned and trotted back into the living room, then up the stairs to the second floor.

Rachel listened a moment; the house was quiet. Contented of course. Contented they were back. From outside she could hear Paul at work—the rasping scrape of the shovel being pushed into the hard earth. He must have decided to bury the girl very close to the house. For his own reasons. His private reasons.

I don't misjudge you, Paul. I love you. And I trust you. But I don't know you. So how can I misjudge you?

It was a good question. A good thought.

She went into the living room, settled into Paul's winged-back chair and waited.

I knew you better before we came here.

But she *did* trust him. She had to; it was not as if she had a choice in the matter.

Well, she could walk, of course. She'd done a lot of walking in New York City, before her marriage to Paul. From Seventy-fifth to Grand Central—over thirty blocks; she'd done that a dozen times or more, and often on a hot summer afternoon, hotter, she thought, in that city than anywhere else on earth. But it was better than the buses, and the subway had always been out of the question. In that respect, she supposed, she would never be a New Yorker, never willing to shut herself up with the crowds unless it was absolutely necessary, which it seldom had been.

The crowds. They had been, she reflected, one of the reasons she had not given Paul a harder time when he'd announced his plans to move to the house. She could have flatly refused, it might have worked, though it would have done irreparable damage to their new marriage. But the crowds. What was it about the great masses of New Yorkers that unsettled her more than other crowds did? Their aloofness? That was part of it. And their very *numbers*. Or, on second thought, perhaps not. Perhaps it was more their aloofness than their numbers. An aloofness that was as if, as New Yorkers—outside their apartments and homes —in the midst of, a part of, or, more correctly, pieces of that creature called New York City, their existence was designed to sustain it, to nourish it. Individuals did not exist in any crowd, but, in New York, the crowd *was* the individual.

And what of the crowds here at the house? Around it.

She remembered a Sunday early in spring that she and Paul had left New York and driven several hundred miles to a little park near Albany. They had supposed that because it was a cool day, and overcast, the park would be theirs alone, until they saw the cars, and the couples moving slowly over the park lawns, in and out of the woods, some with newly procured walking sticks in hand. Still, they thought, there was enough of the park that they'd be able to find a place somewhere that the people, and the sounds of the people, would be behind them.

They walked, avoiding the paths, carefully through thickets, up and down small wooded hills, until they found themselves at a shallow odorless swamp. They paused there. Listened. Nothing. It was a good spot. Who, after all, would avoid the paths, as they had done? It was a perfect spot, free, even, of the occasional beer can or cigarette butt common to the most secluded areas of all parks.

And then they heard the shout of some anxious mother whose child had apparently wandered beyond her control. They looked. The woman was at the top of a high ridge behind them. "Have you seen," the woman called, and she went on to describe her son.

There had been a lesson in that, Rachel thought, though she could not think what it might be. Probably something trite about the encroachment of civilization—that no matter how unspoiled, how wild a place might be, it was wild and unspoiled only because man decreed that it should be that way. If he should decree otherwise . . .

And what of the crowds here at the house? Crowds? The children? Lumas (who, though dead, still occupied the land)? The children did not constitute a crowd. That was silly. They were . . . a part of this place, a part of this creature, just as New Yorkers were a part of the creature called New York. In New York, she was a trespasser. And here too. But there was a difference. Numbers didn't matter. Numbers only . . .

Paul had stopped working.

She sat bolt upright in the chair, listened. She heard, for the first time, the sudden breeze moving over the house, but not that hideous scraping of the shovel.

And, she knew, she had not heard it for some time.

She stood, ran to the bedroom window, pushed the curtain aside, looked out. She had been sure that was where he'd been—beyond this window, close to the house. The scrape of a shovel, like the noise of a rake on hard earth, is a very directional thing.

She listened again. Maybe Paul had merely decided on some other spot, farther away from the house. Maybe he knew that the noise his awful work produced was putting her on edge . . .

She listened hard. Heard only the breeze buffeting the house. The cat tearing about in the upstairs hallway.

And then a sharp, metallic, whumping sound—the car's hood being slammed shut. As if in anger.

She hesitated; perhaps the sound had not been that at all, perhaps something else—. But she could think of nothing that would approximate it.

Before she reached the front porch she knew what

156

Paul would tell her. And how she would react. How she *had*—as her role, or because there was always a question, a doubt, a chance—to react.

He was coming down the lawn from the car when he saw her appear on the front steps.

"Bad news," he said, an embarrassed grin on his face.

Rachel saw that he was holding something in his hand. He held it up. "Part of the fuel line," he told her. He was within a couple yards of her now.

She looked incredulously at the thick, short, black rubber hose. He bent it to expose a slit running at right angles to the length of the hose. "Worn all to hell," he explained.

"Can you fix it, Paul?"

He studied the hose a moment, shrugged his shoulders. "I don't know. Maybe. If I can find some plastic tape, it might work till we get to town. And it might not. I don't know." He shoved the hose into the right pocket of his denim jacket.

"Can we . . . walk, Paul?"

"No real need. Today, at least. And besides, there's a storm coming. Tomorrow, maybe, if I can't fix . . ."

"Tomorrow?"

"Early. Weather permitting." A pause. "You might as well get a fire started in there, it's getting cold." He nodded at the house.

"So we're going to stay." More a statement than a question.

"Just as long as is necessary, Rachel. No longer." Another pause. "I'm sorry."

"So am I, Paul."

He looked questioningly at her a second—*part of his role*—then started around the side of the house. "I'll be finished in an hour or so," he called over his shoulder. And he was gone.

CHAPTER 20

Mundane things—pots, pans, silverware. Cream-colored plates with simple blue borders. Living things—things to live with, to store away in cupboards, to display if they were attractive enough, if there was a place to display them. And, if so, they brightened a place up, if the place needed it, and if the colors were right.

"I don't know; it might be a few days, Rae. There's some bad weather coming in and I'd hate to try that damned road . . ."

A mundane thing. Bad weather. And cozying up inside an old house to be away from it.

"Why don't you . . ."

Ferreting out a lie. A mundane thing. Simple ability. Living was a mundane thing.

"That box in the car; I'll bring it in. We're going to have to eat, you know."

Cream-colored plates on end, all in a line. It made a house a home. And pots and pans, ugly as they were, hung again from ugly nails; so nicely utilitarian.

"We'll be calling this place home a little while longer, Rae. Not much longer, I promise."

Promises.

"Might as well bring the blankets in, too."

And the pillows.

"And the pillows."

Warm beds and a warm fire and cream-colored plates all in a line.

"I hate it, Rae. Keeping you here like this, I mean. I really do. But it can't be helped, can it?"

"If you say so, Paul."

"Well, yes"—big apologetic smile—"I do. I'm sorry."

Ferreting out a lie. It was easy enough. Easier than building one. That was the balance of a lie, and it was a good balance.

"How's this, Paul?" Point smilingly, trembling, at the cream-colored plates all in a line. Help him build the lie.

"That's nice. You should have done that before. It brightens the place up."

Love was a mundane thing. So was trust. Trust was very much like the cream-colored plates. Trust was simple and beautiful and . . .

"Lock up, Rachel. I'll probably be gone till after dark."

"Where are you going?"

"Out there." A nod to indicate the forest.

"Why, Paul?"

"Why? Well, you know why, now don't you? I mean—"

"Do what you think you have to do, Paul."

"I intend to."

Sweep the cream-colored plates to the floor. They spend a long time breaking. Whole minutes. Long, noisy minutes.

He'd prefer New York now to this. He hadn't thought he would—ever. Long ago, he'd reflected that the winter might strand them at the house for days, weeks, but it would be preferable to an ugly New York City winter.

He'd forgotten the rifle. To hell with it. What would he do with it, anyway? And he hadn't actually forgotten it, only thought, at that moment, that he might need it, that he should have brought it along. But to hell with it.

Rachel *knew*. Well, she thought she knew, she *said* she knew. He should have pressed her on it. But to what purpose? Let her know. It probably comforted her to think she saw through him.

What drives you? Had he whispered the words? Impossible. He would have heard—

This is torture for her. That was another voice; the Voice of Conscience. Let it speak. *This will destroy her; destroy her for you, destroy your marriage.* Let the voice play itself out.

It was played out.

"Goddamn!" He'd said that, he realized. It was okay; curses were okay. (Had it been one of his uncles, a relative anyway, who, after a stroke, could utter only curses? That was interesting. There was some primal truth in that. As pathetic and as laughable as it was. All primal truths were like that. Maybe all truths, by their nature as truths, were primal. He loved Rachel, for instance. But to the point of altruism? *That* much? Did anyone love anyone that much? He would gladly—well, perhaps not gladly, but willingly—sacrifice his life for her. Because, it was obvious, there were some things more important to him than his life. But he would also sacrifice both their lives if something . . . something moved him strongly enough.

What was he thinking? What did it all *mean*? That quick thought, that quick . . . truth.)

He cursed again, deep in his throat. "Shit!" The word carried out to several seconds, a curse on his thoughts, something to make them vapid.

160

The gun—he should have brought the goddamned gun.

Maybe that poor dead girl, Rachel thought, had been the last of them, the last of the line, the last of . . . the family. She grinned, despite herself, at the word. The family—a family of children. It was less than ludicrous.

The last of them, anyway. She had been the fourth. Four. A good round number. Easily managed, easily imagined. Easily managed because it was easily imagined. She imagined four bright spots—lights?—on the black backdrop of her consciousness. Easy enough. Five? A little harder, not much harder. And six—two groupings of three, easier than five. Seven. Eight. Nine. Ten. It broke down at eleven, blurred there, required too much shifting, too much uncertainty. Ten was her limit. It was a good game.

Perhaps she had better sweep up the broken plates before Paul returned. Or perhaps not. Those shards and pieces said a lot, more than she could . . . more than she had the courage to say. He would listen to the broken plates; they spoke for her; he could not argue with, could not attempt to placate, to reassure, to humor, to lie to the broken plates. Those shards and pieces would break through to him.

Was she crying again? For God's sake, what use was there in that? This was the time for strength. Strength.

Maybe Paul was crying, too. Maybe he had left the house to cry. In private.

CHAPTER 21

By first light, all traces of the late evening snowfall had vanished. It was a tentative snowfall—a snowfall testing itself; at its end, what it left on the land would have been barely distinguishable from a heavy, lingering frost. It lay very white and very wet on the roof of the farmhouse and the warmth from within the house, and in the air, transformed, reduced it, killed it.

But is was only the first test, the first battle, and the snow always failed the first test, always lost the first battle so early in the year. Because, for now, its allies were weak and unpredictable.

But the change had begun.

Only the creatures that lived on the land, and in it, were aware that it had begun so soon, and so much in earnest.

Rachel smiled at her reflection in the bathroom mirror. Didn't she look pretty this morning, and wasn't that quite a new thing—not that she looked pretty, but that she could take the time to think so. Her smile broadened: That was nice, appealing. Paul should see it. Well, maybe she'd be in the same mood when he came back to the house. Hopefully soon. There was no reason he should be away long, had been no reason for two weeks, ever since their abortive attempt to leave.

That was one cause for her mood this morning, she knew. The last two quiet weeks. Tense weeks, certainly. At least in the first few days, when she had expected . . . anything. Those had been bad days, terrible days. The worst of her life. But they had come and gone and had brought nothing but an awful anticipation of what might happen the following day. Today, that anticipation had, at last, vanished. And she was pretty once again, could take the time to think so once again. *Pretty*, and all that mundane word encompassed.

Premonition, second sight, intuition—damn! whatever it was, whatever it had been, it meant nothing. Happily nothing. The last two quiet weeks proved that.

She ran her comb slowly through her hair, encountering numerous snarls. She worked the comb firmly through them, grimacing now and then at the small pain they produced. Even such personal amenities as this, she thought, had been all but forgotten in the last two weeks. Not forgotten entirely because Paul—damn him! God bless him!— had been there to remind her:

"No. Nothing. Not a sign of them, Rae." And then a pause. "You look terrible. Can't you do something" . . . "with your hair" . . . "with your nails" . . . et cetera, et cetera.

Paul—tower of strength, hardly affected at all by what had happened, by what had not happened, by what could have happened. Definitely the stronger of the two of them, at least lately.

163

Because, in retrospect, it was obvious that much of his strength had been false, had been a show, an act for her benefit.

Like the first night. She so quiet, seated for hours in her wicker chair, a book at her feet (she had given up, almost immediately, any pretense of reading it). And her one question, repeated every fifteen minutes or so, because his answers meant nothing to her:

"Why, Paul?"

He, smiling benevolently each time, variously answering her question from his winged-back chair, from the window that overlooked the fields, from the kitchen while he made coffee for them both, or while pacing the length of the living room (slowly, pointedly, as if in thought, not out of anxiety or apprehension).

"Why? Because we're running from . . . ghosts, aren't we! Letting ghosts drive us away from something we've both wanted for a long time. Something that could be very, very good for us?

Why? "It's all so simple, Rae. We've . . . overreacted. Have they—and that word encompasses a lot, doesn't it?— have they really *done* anything to us? Any harm, I mean? Physical harm? No. And how could they, for God's sake. They're only children."

Why? "I believe it's the best thing, that's why. It will . . . strengthen us."

I don't know why, Rachel. I wish I did, but I don't. Something is . . . pushing me, pushing me, and I'm frightened, Rae. But he never said that, only projected it, wore it so plainly on his face—his stiff, forced smile was part of it, and his gaze so desperately seeking hers was part of it, and his at first hesitant, then strong embrace—*Stay with me, Rae. Protect me, I'll protect you, protect me!*—when they finally went to bed that night.

164

And then, the second day, his morning walks had begun. Her protestations were easily overcome:

"Listen, this is supposed to be a *life* we're living here. This is supposed to be our home, for Christ's sake! Let's not make it our prison."

That had been convincing, because she *had* been making it her prison. And not an assuredly secure one, at that—all the evidence proved it. But there were walls here, and windows, rugs, chairs, cans of soup and cartons of butter in the kitchen, and electricity, however primitive, coursing through the house. Man had built the house, and sustained it. The threat that existed here—if it indeed still did exist—was more of a threat outside it, beyond the walls and windows.

Such thoughts had given her a modicum of comfort when Paul left her in the mornings. But, for the first week —when he had come back with "nothing" . . . "not a sign of them, Rae."—had, progressively, given her less and less comfort. Because they were *waiting!* She knew it. They were *lulling us into a sense of complacency*. It had been an irrational fear which, she realized now, Paul had also succumbed to.

Because there had been the secretive night walks as well. Up at one or two—when he felt certain she was asleep —over to the living room window for a few minutes, then out the back door until three or four in the morning.

The night walks had ended in the middle of the second week. His exhaustion had stopped them—exhaustion coupled, no doubt, with his failure to find anything to sustain his fear.

And that had been when that subtly expressed fear had ended.

Rachel smiled again, encountering a particularly nasty snarl at the same time; the smile remained, the pain registered in her eyes.

"Damn," she whispered through her smile. If only life involved . . . no more pain than this.

It had been like a high fever slowly weakening. Like waiting for bad news which refused to arrive—it was always easier, smarter, to believe that it was only late in coming. And, at last, there came a time when such negativism had—for the good of the organism—to reverse itself. If just temporarily. If only to allow a chance to breathe.

That was today. It had been obvious on her face, in her eyes—the new, bright hope. So easy to read, even while she was still struggling out of sleep.

"Rachel," Paul whispered. "Dear Rachel." She had become, by slow degrees, so patient, so trusting, so adaptable. Really quite an amazing woman, so willing to be . . . his wife—to be protected by him, soothed by him, reassured by him. It had been difficult, almost impossible, at first, but would now be easier, would now be merely the way things were. The way things should have been from the beginning of their lives here.

With his free hand, Paul unbuttoned his denim jacket. The morning's unusual warmth had caused a sticky, uncomfortable sweat to form on his chest.

Dear Rachel. She was that, wasn't she? And more. She was so deliciously vulnerable.

Rachel remembered one thought from two weeks before—that the house hadn't changed, hadn't metamorphized. And in the context that the thought had come to her, she reflected, it had been silly, hysterical.

But there had indeed been changes, she knew. Slow and subtle changes. But so powerful. Changes in the house, in herself, and in Paul.

This was, for one, no longer just a house, any house—a place to pass through, to spend a few nights in, to have a few meals in. A place, in spite of it, to make love—regardless of all the evidence to the contrary, an artificiality, something outside herself. Not something to live *with*, but something to live *in*.

It was no longer all that.

It had changed, was changing, was becoming a part of her. An extension of herself.

And that was the biggest change in her, wasn't it? She was becoming a part of the house, and it was becoming a part of her. It was a good thing, a very comfortable and secure thing (and maybe it was one of the reasons Paul had done what he did, had brought them back. Because he had felt this way from the beginning).

It was a change which had occurred slowly, in direct proportion to the lessening of her anxiety.

She stepped up to the window that overlooked the fields. She pushed the newly installed curtain aside.

And today, this fine, warm morning, the change was nearly complete.

"This is my home," she murmured, half relishing the phrase, half testing it. *Our* home, she corrected. Our home. A place to love in. *The* place to love in.

That had been the biggest change in Paul, hadn't it? His lovemaking. No, his lovemaking—his ability—had always been good. It was his attitude, his attitude toward her, that had changed. Now, at last—ever since their first time—they were making love together. Not she to him, nor her to her. But together. Only one word—perfection—could describe it. And it had only one goal (how provincial it sounded; but it was true), a goal which had somehow damnably eluded her in the last six months. Now, there was hope, that goal would be realized.

"I love you, Paul," she said. "I love you so much." She frowned. This was a bit foolish, talking this way, as if the spirit of her words could somehow traverse the physical distance between them. But, hell, if anyone was entitled to such foolishness . . .

She let the curtain fall, crossed to the bedroom and glanced at the alarm clock on the dresser: 11:45. He'd be home soon; he should have been home by 11:30. That, after all, had been his schedule since they'd come back . . .

Paul had, finally, to admit it. He was lost. Of course, it was bound to happen, and it wasn't as if he hadn't been warned. Marsh had warned him, and so had Lumas, more than once:

"Don't get careless, Paul. We get people like you—city folk, I mean—hunters, they are—we get 'em up in these parts every year. Seems like hundreds of 'em all stumbling through the woods, thinking they're such great trackers and all. And it never fails; one or two of 'em—every year it happens, seems like—one or two of 'em gets lost. And I don't mean for a few hours, or a day. I mean *lost*. For good. They get excited by a deer spore or whatever and go running off without giving no thought to where they been or where they are or how they got there, and before they know it, they look around and nothin's familiar, like suddenly they been put on another planet or somethin'. And soon enough, they panic. When that happens, forget it. Oh, some get lucky and find themselves on a path or a road after a while. But most don't. A lot don't. Shit, there must be a whole village full of lost half-wit hunters around here by now."

The first step, Paul knew, was to mentally retrace his route. To be sure of it, 110 percent sure. Half sure, fairly sure, wasn't good enough. And to be *sure* he was sure. Certain of it. How many, he wondered, have rationalized themselves into oblivion? (And that—the thought—was a good beginning.)

168

He looked about again, again as if casually, critically. He frowned. Another planet indeed. It was the same planet. It had been merely . . . rearranged.

This was the woods he had known, had walked a thousand times. Of course! His perspective was wrong. Perspective was everything, wasn't it?

So, the first step, the real first step, was to change his perspective.

He turned, faced the way he had come. And saw his footprints; moist, dark, having exposed the shallow underlayers of decayed leaves and pine needles. He followed the prints with his eyes—up the slight, tree-covered hill. He drew a quick breath, held it. Damn it, goddammit! He would have remembered coming down that hill. He would have remembered.

He tried hard to remember. And remembered only the other hill, a little steeper than this one; he had nearly fallen down it, had stopped the fall by grabbing hold of and almost uprooting a very young pine, had gotten one of its needles stuck in the fleshy part of his left hand. There was, he noticed for the first time, a dull ache in that hand now.

That near fall was when he had begun to lose himself. To become disoriented. To know it, and at the same time, out of pride, to deny it.

And that denial of his own incompetence (clumsiness? stupidity?) had also erased what should have been an easy recollection.

Because he could not remember coming down this hill.

Or going back up it.

And down again. As the other, parallel sets of footprints told him he had done.

And he could not remember what his eyes had shown him at the top of that hill. More of the same, obviously—rolling, tree-studded brown hills, snaking underbrush, all lighted randomly by yellow shafts of morning sunlight.

Nothing of importance. No recognizable landmarks. Otherwise he would not have come down again. That was logical enough.

Dear Mom,

It's been a long time, I know. I should have written before this, and I'm sorry. I am, I really am.

You will have to get down here soon; I think you'd like it. I know *I* do. It's not that I've *learned* to like it, or that I've forced myself to like it. It's that it's grown on me. I'm beginning to feel that this is where I belong—maybe that this is where I'll stay. Don't get me wrong. It's rough, very rough, and I suppose there's still a good possibility that we'll give it up. But— Well, we'll have to wait, won't we? Wait and see.

Paul sends his love. He's working very hard getting this place ready for winter. It's not insulated, of course, and there are no storm windows, etc., but he's piling firewood up at the back of the house, and putting plastic over the windows and doors, and sealing all those places where the cold can get in. He complains, of course, but I think he secretly enjoys it. Man against the elements and all that.

We were going to leave a few weeks ago. We *did* leave. But Paul brought us back. I'm glad—it comforts me that he did.

He's a strong man. He's a wonderful man, Mother.

And because he belongs here, so do I. That's where we've gotten with

Paul turned again. A quarter turn. From where he now stood the downslope of the hill continued at a casual angle another fifty feet; it terminated at an all-but-dry stream bed. Just beyond that, a flat half-circular clearing fringed by closely spaced deciduous trees, some, at random, completely bare, but most still holding their full complement of leaves—now, with autumn upon them, bright shades of red and yellow and brown.

Paul grimaced. Perspective again. He had obviously been facing a slightly different direction before turning to face the hill behind him. Otherwise he would have seen this clearing. And he was sure he hadn't.

"For Christ's sake!" he whispered. He was about to whisper it again when something small, something slightly off-white glinted dully at him from the clearing.

He moved forward hesitantly. Stepped easily across the stream bed. Stopped a few yards from the edge of the clearing. His brow creased. "What the . . ."

The bones were everywhere. Some threw pinpoints of sunlight at him, some were barely visible in the stunted, greenish-yellow grasses.

Paul's head turned slowly, steadily, as he studied the clearing. A full minute.

Then his muscles relaxed as realization came to him.

It was suddenly so deadeningly obvious.

This was a feeding ground. It was a dinner table. *Their* dinner table.

His hands began to quiver slightly, uncontrollably.

What in God's name brought him here? It had to have been something.

Then with greater force, spreading to his arms.

He could almost remember. It was there—the memory —at the edge of his consciousness. Something.

And his entire body shook, as if it had been caught, naked, in an unbelievably cold wind.

Talk? Had there been talk? Yes. Voices. And laughter.

Children at play. Children amusing themselves. Children being amused. But that, he knew at once, was not what brought him here.

There *had* been voices. And laughter. But not the voices of children, and not their laughter. His brain had been trying desperately for something familiar, something sweet and benign.

And then his body was quiet. Still. At rest.

Because it was his own voice, his own laughter, Rachel's voice, and Rachel's laughter, that had brought him here. Had led him here.

To the feeding ground. The dinner table.

"Oh, Christ!"

And the thing deep inside him—asleep so long—shook itself awake. And sought release. It probed about again in his arms, his legs, his belly. It gnawed at his brain and the backs of his eyes. Pushed him—pushed Paul Griffin—back. To the beginning. To the birth. And Paul Griffin fought it, slammed it down, took his place again, briefly, in the present. Then, longer now, it was once again the beginning, then, for an instant, Elizabeth Griffin lay silently before him. And her husband wept. And, again, the present. And then the beginning. And, at last—and for long enough —the two merged, coalesced.

And Paul Griffin turned quietly, sharply, to his left. Thirty minutes later, he was home.

CHAPTER 22

OCTOBER 23

Rachel studied the rough-cut pine and oak logs. She pursed her lips. It would never do. The pile was too high, too narrow. It was not the way she had seen wood piled up before. Not in these little lopsided pyramids. It was a waste of space. Why not a straight pile spanning the length of the cellar wall? That was the way it should be done, the way, in fact, that Paul had begun it. Until, the day before:

"It seems so . . . so asymmetrical. You know what I mean, Rae."

"Asymmetrical?"

"I guess what I mean is, what I mean is—it's too logical, it's too rational, too cold."

"Oh. You want it to be arty, is that it?"

"Arty? No. I guess I want it to be . . . warmer. I guess I want it to be—you know." He paused, searched for the right word.

"Inviting?" Rachel offered.

"Yes. Inviting! How about; I mean, how about if you stack them up like this."

And he had taken the next hour—and three tries—to build the first lopsided pyramid. It pleased him:

"Like that, Rae," he said, smiling. "Like that."

"Yes," she sighed. "I see."

"Good. Well, pile the rest of the wood up the same way, okay? And keep the piles the same distance from one another. It won't take long, I promise."

Inviting, for God's sake! This—she had built five pyramids; enough wood remained, she supposed, to build two more—was about as inviting as a fortress, or a bee farm (yes, that's what the pyramids reminded her of; beehives, the kind men built).

Paul worked slowly, methodically, letting the ax do the work. It was the way, he remembered, his father had taught him; "The tree will wait." Only a day's practice had brought it all back; "Slow and easy, son. Slow and easy."

It was almost like making love, felling a tree. The first bite of the ax was the approach, testing the territory. And the second and third bite—that was wearing the resolve away. Then, at the middle . . .

He let the metaphor dissipate. It was distasteful, comparing life and death that way. The only similarity was the reverence with which each had to be approached. And the power of each. And the dependence of one on the other. This tree had to die so that he and Rachel could be comfortable (could protect themselves from the murderous winter).

It was a birch, one of dozens in an acre-sized grove just north of the forest, off his land, he realized, but it didn't matter. The grove was very old; within a year, blight or insects would get it. Or weather. Better it was put to good use. Better that it helped to warm him, them. Rachel and him.

Because that was the only consideration now, wasn't it? Surviving the winter. Keeping the cold air out of the house. And the warm air in. Keeping food in the cupboards and meat in the refrigerator. And love (in the bedroom) within them both and (in the living room) surviving the first storm, which was not far off—it was in the air; the feel of it—and hoping spring would come early, and knowing it wouldn't, because it never had, not here (in the backyard, on the porch).

The tree cracked. It was less than a half foot in diameter and Paul had spent only a short while on it. He stepped back, anticipating the angle of its fall. Another crack, louder than the first, moister. The tree leaned back, almost imperceptibly, then forward and slightly to the left. Then it fell. Softly. Undramatically.

Paul set to work on it immediately, cutting it into easily transportable sections. It would be the last for this load, he decided. The makeshift carrier he'd fashioned from half-inch plywood and two-by-fours and attached, with a chain, to the back of the tractor, was already straining under the weight of just a half morning's work.

(Good work.

Nature's work.)

He'd go home. He'd have some lunch. He'd spend some time, a few minutes, with Rachel.

He'd come back here till evening.

It was good, Rachel thought, so very good to feel this way about the house, at last. She knew it was coming. Even when they were leaving! Which had been the reason for her pointed questions: *Why are we leaving, Paul?* And *Why are we staying, Paul?*

Because the magic was here. Magic. In the old walls, and in the land. And in herself. It had been given to her.

Dear Mother,
I wanted to write this letter particularly

She paused, uncertain how to explain, in words, what had happened to her, the magic. It would be hard to say without sounding fatuous, though no one's skepticism, not even her mother's, could matter very much, now.

because I have much I want to say and I don't know how to say it and I want you to understand.

As if even she—Rachel—could understand. An infant doesn't make the effort to understand why its mother's touch makes it feel good, it merely enjoys. (But that wasn't too apt a comparison, was it? Because she *did* want to know. Not passionately, just out of curiosity, if only to assure herself that the magic would last.)

I want us both to understand. In a sentence—I'm certain Paul and I are going

Daylight through the front window was cut off suddenly. Rachel reached out and switched the lamp on.

to stay. For good (I hope. It's Paul's decision ultimately, you see. But I think he feels the way I do). We're getting electricity and a telephone by the end of the month, and that will certainly help. I could suffer through a pioneer existence another two weeks, I imagine (Paul had me stacking firewood this morning) before climbing the walls.

She felt something at her feet. She looked. It was the cat, purring and kneading the rug and looking contentedly up at her.

"Yes," Rachel said, "I'll put in a word or two about you, don't worry." The cat meowed softly, then wandered away toward the bedroom.

I'm still waiting for you to pay us a visit. You'll see quickly enough why I've taken to this place, why it's worked its magic

(there, got the word in)

on me. And on Paul. And on Mr. Higgins (who would live nowhere else).

I keep asking myself, was it only a couple weeks ago that I was so dead set on

The desk was suddenly awash with light. Rachel glanced to her left, out the window. She turned back to the letter. To whom had she been writing? she wondered. And what had she been writing?

"Dear Mother," she read aloud. "I wanted to write this letter particularly because I have much I want to say" . . . She studied the letter quizzically a moment. She set it on the desk. Much she wanted to say? Why to her mother? She had said all she wanted to say to Paul, who was the only one who really mattered, or cared.

She crumpled the letter and dropped it into the wastebasket to the left of the desk. She stood, crossed the living room, went into the bathroom. She went over to the tub, turned the water on, tested it.

EVENING

"So that's what I mean, Paul. I feel good about this house. I feel . . ."

177

"Secure?"

"That's a little off of the right word. I don't know if there *is* a right word. Secure? Yes, though not strictly in the sense of . . . what? Safety? Out of danger? I never felt physically in danger. Though, looking back, that probably doesn't mean very much."

"Uh-huh."

"I feel I'll be able to live here. With you. That *we'll* be able to live here."

"And all that has happened?"

"Is behind us, Paul. All of that is behind us. It's painful to remember it. I'm not going to pretend it isn't. It's very painful. But I guess the trick is . . . is *to* remember it. To try to look at it objectively."

"Can you do that, Rachel?"

"I'll give it a try."

"Will you?"

"Yes. When I can. And with your help."

"My help?"

"Guidance. That's a silly word, and I'm sorry for it. But it's what I want from you. It's what I feel you can give me, whether you know it or not."

"Ha! Just call me 'Father Griffin.' "

"I'm serious, Paul. Please don't joke."

"Sorry."

A long pause.

"Are you surprised, Paul?"

"Surprised? At what?"

"At this . . . abrupt turnaround in my attitude?"

"It wasn't really that abrupt. I could see it—I saw it coming. You probably didn't even realize it, that it was coming. I guess you just had to be persuaded. I guess you had to persuade yourself. That sounds pretty cryptic, doesn't it, but it's true. You stay here long enough and despite every thing, this place grows on you."

178

"Yes, I know, it becomes . . ."

"And, really, all things considered, it beats the hell out of New York. And we'll work out the problems we've still got. You'll see. It's just a matter of time."

"Well, we'd have problems wherever we were, Paul. It's not a matter of degree, it's a matter of kind. And I think I prefer the kind that face us now."

"Glad to hear it. I really am. Because we've got all kinds of problems."

"I know it."

"Do you?"

"Yes. I just wanted you to know—this house, everything . . . all of it feels good."

CHAPTER 23

Ellen Thruston knew she shouldn't be here, in this car. Gary Hallock's car. She'd been warned about Gary Hallock—"He'll eat you alive," Jackie told her, "and then—" Raised eyebrows, a nod of the head: *He'll spit you out.* She hadn't needed to say it. Everyone knew about Gary Hallock. What he lacked in brains—one of these years he would finally graduate, then maybe the army could take him. Maybe—he tried to make up for in cock work. Tried? Succeeded! Practically every willing girl in the school had had him—been had by him—at least once. And there was no lack of willing girls at Penn Yan High.

Ellen half wished he wouldn't hold her so tightly while he drove. The road was bad, a dirt road, and it seemed only with great reluctance that he had brought the car's speed down from seventy-five, on the paved road, to slightly less than fifty here. The old car rattled and whined like it was on its last breath.

"Gary," she said, "don't you think . . ."

But he hadn't heard her. The noise of the engine and the wind rushing past the open windows meant she would have to shout, and she wasn't up to that.

She leaned over, said into his ear, "Gary, can we stop soon?"

Gary Hallock grinned—machismo, expectation, a dash of idiocy. He was not really a handsome man, Ellen thought. He was . . . intriguing; dark, tallish, with a lot of hair, but not too much of it.

"Sure," he said. "Sure, Can't wait, huh?"

Ellen smiled an affirmative smile.

Gary slowed the car to thirty, negotiated a sharp left hand turn skillfully, punched the car up to fifty again.

Yes, Ellen told herself, *This was probably a mistake.* But it was too late, thankfully, far too late, now to correct it. She wondered briefly how many of the other girls had had the same—albeit weak—misgivings; or was she somehow superior to them, somehow, in the end, more discriminating?

". . . could go in there," Gary was saying. He jerked his head to the left. "What do ya think?"

Ellen looked; they were approaching an old farmhouse; an upper window was boarded up, the front yard was a mass of weeds; to the casual observer it had all the signs of abandonment.

"What if someone lives there?" Ellen said.

"Aw, shit," Gary began. "What do ya mean?" He took his foot off the accelerator, let the car slow to twenty-five, pushed the brake pedal hard. Ellen reached out instinctively, put her open hand against the dashboard, although Gary had strengthened his hold on her. "There ain't nobody livin' there," he went on. "Who the fuck would live there?"

They were almost in front of the house now.

"I don't know," Ellen said. "I just think . . ."

Then both of them saw the woman; she was behind the front door, she could see them, they knew. But she was looking straight ahead, at the road.

Gary and Ellen watched her for a few seconds.

"Let's go, Gary."

"Yeah, I guess." And, surprising Ellen, he touched the accelerator slowly, and rolled past the house at a safe, slow speed.

She looked quizzically at him. After a moment, and with effort, he grinned. "Don't wanna disturb the lady in her meditations, do we?" He paused briefly.

"Road ends up here," he went on. "We'll stop there. We'll have some fun. That all right with you?" He chuckled.

And yes, it was quite all right, quite, quite all right. Perfect. *Hurry it up, please.*

And Gary again brought the car to a quick halt. He turned the ignition off, looked around. There were sunlit, yellow fields to either side of the road, and ahead, and to the west, at the horizon, a small, dark pine forest.

"Nice, huh?" Gary said.

A honeybee, logy in the cool air, bounced against the windshield a few times.

"Can we roll the windows up?" Ellen asked.

"You roll 'em up, I gotta take a piss." He opened his door. "I'll be right back. You can get those clothes off in the meantime." He nodded at Ellen's green, bulky sweater and white Levi's. Ellen grabbed the bottom of her sweater with both hands, lifted, exposed her breasts, hesitated.

She felt his eyes on her, enjoyed it. She pulled the sweater over her head. "Like that," she said, throwing the sweater into the back seat.

"Yeah," he said, "like that." He got out of the car, leaned over, stared, grinning, at her breasts for a long moment. "Keep 'em warm," he said; he turned and moved into the fields.

Ellen waited. When only the back of his head was visible above the tall weeds, she unbuttoned the Levi's,

slid the zipper down, pushed the pants, and her underwear, to below her knees. She hesitated, certain she had
heard something on the road behind the car. She turned,
looked. Nothing. She turned back, slipped out of the pants
and underwear, threw them onto the back seat.

She sat quietly for a moment, she glanced to her left.
Hurry up, she wanted to call, wonderfully, ecstatically,
aware of the moisture collecting between her legs, of the
warm, tingling sensation in her breasts. She turned slightly
to the right. She closed her eyes, she waited, body bent
forward, hands between her thighs. *Hurry up*, she thought.

She heard the car door open. She opened her eyes.

"Well, it's about time," she whispered. She started to
turn to face the door. Stopped. Enjoyed the warm hand on
her breast. "That feels good," she murmured. She closed
her eyes again. Felt the other hand come around and cup
her right breast. "That feels so good, Gary."

"Gotta take a piss," she heard.

The hands left her breasts, pushed her head gently
toward the passenger door, descended, to her waist, lifted
her, set her down so she was lying on her stomach on the
car seat. She spread her legs.

"Gotta take a piss," she heard again. She wished
vaguely that he would stop saying it; it almost spoiled the
mood. Almost.

"Do it, Gary."

And Gary screamed; a harsh, tortured, fear-ridden
scream. A scream at a distance. From the fields.

Ellen froze.

The hands left her.

"Gary?" she whispered.

She heard the screams repeated.

She scrambled to a sitting position, instinctively
reached for her clothes on the back seat, saw a mound of
dark hair through the back window.

183

Another scream. Closer. Louder.

Naked, clothes in hand, she threw her door open and got out of the car.

"Oh, Jesus, Jesus," Gary shouted. He screamed again. Ellen pulled her sweater on.

"Gary?" she called. "Gary, what's the matter, Gary?" *What's happening here?! Oh, God, what is happening here?*

Gary appeared suddenly at the side of the road. His pants were bunched up at his ankles. He was clutching his right thigh and half hopping, half stumbling toward her. Ellen could see blood around his hands.

"Gary! My God, Gary—"

"I been bit. Somethin' bit me. Bad!" And he collapsed.

Ellen ran to him, bent over, pulled his hands away from his thigh. She screamed. Stood. Ran to the car, hesitated, looked back. Gary had regained consciousness, had pushed himself to his feet, was stumbling toward her. She watched him a moment, unable to move. She ran to him, helped him to the car, put him in the driver's seat.

"Gary, someone—someone—"

"Damn you, bitch. Get in the fuckin' car. I gotta get to a fuckin' doctor."

She ran around to the passenger side, noted, briefly, that, like Gary—whose pants had come off completely when he had struggled to his feet—she was naked from the waist down, thought, more briefly, how foolish they would look if they were stopped, and got in.

Gary started the car and executed a quick K-turn. He slammed the accelerator to the floor.

Three miles south of the house, on a particularly narrow section of the road, Gary again lost consciousness. Ellen screamed, and watched as the gully came up at them.

She thought how slow the whole process—death—really was.

Rachel put her hands on the sides of the chair, locked her arms, pressed down. Well, the chair didn't creak and shiver, at least. It would probably hold her.

She adjusted the chair under the back window, checked the alignment. She picked up the hammer and a nail from the floor, put one foot on the chair seat. And paused. She was forgetting something, she knew. But what? She thought a moment. The curtain rod; she had to get that measurement right before she put any nails into the window frame. She took her foot off the chair seat and glanced around the room. The curtain rod, the curtain, all those little fixtures; she had laid them out somewhere earlier that morning. Right here in the living room, she thought.

She crossed to her desk, flicked the light on, studied the room carefully. No curtain, no curtain rod, no fixtures.

"Damn," she whispered.

Then she remembered. Paul had laid everything out for her the previous evening. In the kitchen. On the kitchen table. But she had been in there to fix coffee earlier, and to get the chair, and she didn't remember . . .

She took a couple steps to her right. It was all there, she saw, on the kitchen table. Her coffee cup, too.

She sighed. This was becoming routine—forgetting things. Especially in the morning, especially within an hour or so after waking, before she had been able to build a good fire in the fireplace. Yesterday morning it had been, *Did I have breakfast yet?* And the morning before that, when she had been upstairs putting clear plastic over the bedroom windows, it had been, *Did I build a fire?* The question had gnawed at her while she worked and she eventually had to go downstairs to answer it.

She went into the kitchen, gathered the curtain, rod, and fixtures into her arms, and went back to the window. She set the curtain and fixtures on the floor and, rod in hand, stepped up on the chair.

She found, as she worked, that she was humming. It pleased her. It meant something—that she was contented, that she was happy. And the little things—like the memory loss; and that dull ache in her breasts and around her thighs, an ache that had been with her for a week or so— had not altered the contentment. There were even times that inexplicably, it all seemed interconnected—the ache, the memory loss, the contentment (magic). As if one followed the other in succession.

She did not recognize the tune she hummed. It was certainly a very simple melody; it could, she thought, have easily been a chant, a Gregorian chant maybe.

She finished putting the rod up, stepped off the chair, and checked the alignment again. Satisfied that the rod was straight, she picked up the curtain and got back up on the chair.

She heard the front door open.

She looked toward it, startled. Paul appeared in the living room doorway.

"Hi," he said. He took his coat off, threw it on the kitchen table, and came over to her. He put his hands on her waist.

"Hi," she said. "What are you doing home so early?"

"Early?" he said, lifting her a few inches and setting her down on the floor.

She turned to face him. He kissed her softly on the forehead.

"Yes," she said. She paused. "It can't be much past twelve."

"Twelve? No, it's closer to four o'clock, Rachel." He checked his wristwatch. "Three fifty-six, to be exact."

"It can't be, Paul. I mean, I just woke up a couple hours ago."

"You slept pretty late, didn't you?" It was an accusation.

"No, Paul. I woke up at seven-thirty. I remember looking at the alarm clock. I remember that."

He chuckled shortly. "Do you mean that you've misplaced, what—four hours?"

She raised her eyebrows: "Apparently I have," she said.

He stepped away from her and gave her a slow once-over, as if what she had done with the four hours was printed somewhere on her body.

"You've been outside, Rae, I can tell you that."

She looked quizzically at him. "Outside? No, I haven't."

"Look at your arms," he said.

"My arms?"

"Look at them."

She held her arms up.

"You didn't have those scratches this morning," Paul told her.

"My God, Paul." A whisper. "I don't remember . . . I have no idea—"

She was wearing one of Paul's flannel shirts with the sleeves rolled up. Short, narrow, barely visible scratches crisscrossed the outside of both forearms.

"It's some kind of rash, Paul. It has to be. I did *not* go outside today, I know I didn't."

"You must have . . ."

"Wait a minute," she interrupted. An image had flashed through her consciousness; sunlit fields, the house, a long distance off, cut by tall grasses—vaguely, as if seen through a clouded, fish-eye lens. "Wait a minute," she repeated, the image reappearing, clearer. She smiled. "Yes," she continued, "I remember now. I woke up, I got dressed, I went outside." She paused again. "I went down that path. Yes. I went down it, then I went into those fields to the north. And then." Another pause.

"Yes," Paul coaxed. "Go on."

"And then I . . . I went to sleep. I took a nap. I went outside and took a damned nap."

Paul laughed shortly again. "You're really getting into living here, aren't you? It was pretty cold today, do you remember that?"

"No," she answer immediately. "No, I remember being very warm, very comfortable."

"Well, that's okay too," Paul said. He stepped forward, put his arms around her. He drew his head back a little. "What's this?" he said. He gently coaxed something out of her hair, held it up for her to see. "A burr," he said.

"Uh-huh," she said. She put her head against his shoulder. "Paul," she began, "I'm a little frightened. Not remembering like this—"

"You remembered. You told me all about it."

"Don't humor me, Paul. Something's wrong. I don't know, maybe I've got, I don't know, epilepsy or something: I'm a little frightened, Paul. And at the same time I'm so happy, I'm so contented."

"Well, then, that's all that should concern you, Rae. Just . . . enjoy, that's all. So what if your memory's been a little faulty. So what? It's just this house, the land, everything working its . . ."

Magic!

". . . magic on you, that's all. Your mind, your emotions are making a big adjustment, and I, for one, am very pleased by it."

She said nothing.

He stepped away from her. "Now, let me take you out to the car and show you what I got in town today. For

188

one, we'll have no more cold mornings, I got one of those portable electric heaters, if the generator can handle it, only cost me $29.95, it was on sale, and I got a couple gallons of bottled water—we'll use it only for coffee, okay? —and . . ."

She listened, bewildered, at first, as he explained his day's activities, then, as he led her outside, still talking— nonstop talking, so unlike him, she thought, but it was nice—she became aware that she was being caught up in his enthusiasm, almost hypnotized by it. By the time they had brought the heater, the water, a heavy quilt, a dozen paperback books, mostly mysteries, two fifty-pound bags of rock salt, and twenty pounds of various meats ("A lot of it should keep pretty well in the fruit cellar, Rachel") into the house—she noted that she was no longer troubled, no longer frightened at all, that she even felt a little foolish remembering the way she had talked, a little embarrassed, like an adolescent who, trying hard to act like an adult, throws a tantrum, and reflects on it later.

And after they had put everything away and Paul was seated at the table waiting for his dinner, Rachel, at the stove, said matter-of-factly, "Sorry for the way I acted earlier. You can imagine the way I felt."

"Yes, I can," Paul said. "I certainly can. But that sort of thing happens to all of us every now and then. It's nothing to get upset about."

Rachel agreed that it did indeed happen to every-one, though she couldn't think of anyone else it had happened to, and that she was no longer upset. That she was, and had been, and would be, quite comfortable, quite content. Thanks to him.

CHAPTER 24

NOVEMBER 8

It was the first time in weeks that Paul had left her alone at the house. He had said he would the night before; "We're going to have to restock the cupboards, and that means I'll have to go into town tomorrow. It would be helpful if you'd stay here, Rae. I know it's asking a lot, but I think it would be . . . for the best."

She had, surprising herself a little, given him no argument. He would leave her alone at the house; she would stay alone, and that was that. She would merely be certain all the doors and windows were locked. Very simple. No one could get in then.

Paul had left without waking her. Part of his plan, she supposed (if he still felt he needed one, and he probably did; he would always be protective of her. It was only natural, and forgivable and chauvinistic and sweet). God, she loved him. And the changes that had come over him. His temper had all but disappeared, for instance (how he used to scare her with that temper). He was more talkative, sillier, perhaps (an image of the lopsided pyramids came to her) but that was all right, no one needed to spend his life in deadly, smothering seriousness, unwilling to laugh spontaneously or to say stupid things on occasion—such people were obviously afraid of themselves.

She was not sure, however, about his lovemaking, about the direction it had taken in the last couple weeks. For a while, a few days, she remembered, it had been unbelievably good. They had shared each other, their bodies, their love, rather than taken from one another. But there was little or nothing of that sharing left. Something had taken its place. For both of them. Greed, maybe, though that word was, somehow, too civilized, too accusatory, too judgmental. It only scraped the edges, wore away the protective layer. It was impossible to define or even to know what lay beneath. Something very . . . powerful. And that, she knew, accounted for her aching thighs, her aching pelvis, her aching breasts—the power he had brought to their lovemaking. The power she had returned. As if some freedom had suddenly been given to them, a freedom without boundaries. And they were using it.

They. It was that reality which set aside much of her uneasiness about his new lovemaking. Because she had quickly reciprocated. Looked forward to it. Needed it.

She glanced at the old tub and thought how ugly it was, that the water in it smelled bad like a sewer ("It's well water, Rae. Well water always smells like that"). That the room had always been so dismal and unappealing. And she thought, also, how logically, how objectively, she was looking at it, as if she were a visitor or an interior designer and didn't really have to live here.

She slipped out of her nightgown, faced the mirror above the sink. For a few seconds she found herself preoccupied by a web of thin brown lines near the lower right hand corner of the mirror. Then she saw her breasts in the mirorr and smiled. A satisfied smile. These breasts pleased

Paul. And they pleased her. She cupped them gently in her hands, her smile vanished. She studied her face, enjoyed the quiet pleasure registered on it, the quiet power.

She let her hands fall slowly, turned, bent over the tub, put her fingers in the water.

She heard a door being opened somewhere in the house. She cocked her head slowly to one side. Had she locked all the doors? she wondered.

She got into the tub.

Jesus, the water smelled bad. *"It's well water, Rae. It's highly sulfurous."*

Had she locked all the doors yet? she wondered again —distractedly, as if wondering about the birthday of a not-very-close friend. Perhaps she had, perhaps she hadn't.

She heard footfalls—something moving slowly, softly, across the living room, or the bedroom.

"Higgins?" she called. "Higgins," she whispered.

Highly sulfurous. And it smelled bad. And it caressed her so lovingly, as if it could, actually could, caress her, and wanted to.

She let her body relax, let her eyes close, felt her eyelids fluttering, the sides of her lips draw upward.

Her hands moved freely over her body, paused momentarily at her breasts, pressed lightly, lovingly, powerfully. Extensions of the water, like herself.

And then to her belly (a child would be there) to her thighs, to between them, to inside (and out; out there), and loved the water moving in, wanting to move in.

Highly sulfurous. "It smells so bad, Paul" . . . "Just full of minerals, like I said, Rae."

She let her arms relax; they moved slowly to the surface of the water, floated. She let her eyes relax. They opened halfway.

She felt the water being moved. Felt the small warm

hands on her, the thin fingers probing gently, wonderingly, powerfully.

Mike D'Angelo muttered a quick, squeaking obscenity. He was a big man—"Moose" in his high school days—and the obscenity, made high-pitched by fear, did not please him. He tried it again, forcing his voice down; the result was a guttural, rumbling; "Fuckin' shit!" And it pleased him, eased his fear a little.

They're gonna laugh. They were the other members of his hunting party—Bill Russel, Jim McCormick, Sean Weeker, Jack Wilson. They would laugh, they probably were laughing right now. "Don't go wandering off unless you want to be a permanent resident," Bill had told him. Jack had agreed, and Jim had agreed, and Sean, who had known Mike for a number of years, had laughed and said, "Let me tell ya, if anyone's gonna get lost, it'll be him." And then they all laughed.

Mike had, now, to admit that this was a good joke. They knew this country, had hunted here a dozen times. And in a little while they'd come and get him and lead him back to the car and there would be no mention at all of Bill's suggestion that he—Mike—"go over that way"—to the north—"into those woods; I got an eight-pointer in there once."

For sure they were laughing now. Laughing and coming after him because no one leaves a man stranded like this and a joke can go too far, can't it?

If it had been a joke.

If they really did know their way around these woods.

If Bill really did bag an eight-pointer here once.

No. Too many ifs. It had been a joke. There were no ifs about it.

He slid open the bolt on his Winchester 30.06, slipped

a cartridge in, closed the bolt, took the safety off. Just a precaution, he told himself. After all, there were bobcats and foxes around here and sure, they'd probably be more afraid of him than he would be of them, but maybe one would be rabid and not care, or maybe he'd disturb some kittens and their mother, or a vixen and her cubs. Maybe. And it was always better to play it safe.

Like he should have done an hour ago (two hours ago?) when he'd started losing himself, and all because of some vague movement off in the distance in these woods. (Hell, it could have been anything, didn't necessarily have to be a deer just because it was such a quick movement.) He should have called to the others then. That's what he should have done, instead of running off half-cocked. He chuckled suddenly. *Half-cocked,* that was funny! That was awfully damned funny. What was the joke his brother-in-law told him about that? Oh yeah, the detective . . . Mike laughed. Loud and hard.

He stopped laughing abruptly. He stood very still. Was he seeing right? For Christ's sake, was he seeing right?

What in hell was a naked woman doing in these woods? And in November?

He thought of calling to her, but knew the distance was too great, that the brisk, fitful wind pushing through the trees would carry his voice away.

He aimed the rifle at her, peered through the telescopic sight. For sure she was naked, and she was a beauty. Jesus, if a guy was going to get lost, this was one hell of a place to do it.

He grinned, blinked, saw that she had turned, was moving away from him. He lowered the gun slightly. Now, *that* was nice. That was so—

He felt pressure in the small of his back, through his hunting jacket; he whirled. Nothing. He felt pressure at his thighs; a sharp, stinging pain on the calf of his right leg. He swung the rifle back, felt it connect with something soft. The pressure, the stinging pain stopped. He whirled again. "God, God! Bill, Jack—"

"God, God!" he heard. "Bill, Jack—"

He felt the weight on his back. And in the next instant he felt the flesh on the left side of his neck being ripped away.

"Bill," he cried. "Oh, Jesus . . . Jesus!"

"Bill," he heard. "Oh, Jesus . . . Je—"

LATE AFTERNOON

Rachel glanced out the front window for the fifth time in a half hour, hoping to see the car pull up. She sighed. How much longer could he be; all he had to do was pick up some groceries, and maybe do a few errands he hadn't told her about. An hour, at most, for the groceries, another hour for the imagined errands, an hour to and from town. Three hours. If he left around seven, he should have been back by ten, or eleven (at the latest), and here it was four already. She stepped away from the window, folded her arms, tapped her foot rhythmically against the rug. When the phone was put in, he'd have no excuse—

It would be dark by six.

Her foot quieted.

Dark by six. She had never experienced that, darkness and solitude at the house. *That* wasn't something to look forward to. She grimaced, turned again to the window. Nothing. It was true, after all, about the watched pot. It never boiled. And the car you waited for never arrived while you watched for it. If you kept on watching, you'd watch forever because the universe, the status quo, the empty place where the car should be, wouldn't change: Only by divine, and therefore uncontrollable, intervention could it change. And that only happened if you looked away.

She looked away. She stood quietly for a full minute. She looked again. Nothing.

"Dammit," she whispered. She crossed the room to the back window, ran her finger up and down the curtain— "Oh, c'mon, Paul," she said.

And she heard a car pull up. Seconds later, she heard a car door close.

She ran to the front door, threw it open.

But it was not Paul's car.

And the man walking down the lawn wasn't Paul.

The man waved. "Hello," he called, "could I talk to you?"

Rachel looked confusedly at him. She said nothing.

The man mounted the porch steps heavily, opened the porch door. He hesitated. "Could I talk to you, please? It's kind of important." He smiled again; a big, broad, false smile.

"Is it about Paul?" Rachel said. "Has something . . ."

"Paul?" the man interrupted.

"My husband. Paul. He's late."

"Oh," the man said, stepping onto the porch; he held the door open for a second, then closed it slowly. "No." He paused. "May I come in?"

"I'd rather you didn't." She spoke in a monotone. "Paul doesn't like me to let strangers in the house."

The man smiled again, quickly, as if to say he understood. "Well, okay," he began. "My name's Russel. Bill Russel." He waited for Rachel to acknowledge him, to introduce herself. She said nothing. "Yes," he went on. "Russel, I, uh, wanted to ask if maybe you've seen a hunter around here. Big guy, He's wearing a dark blue hunting jacket."

"Yes?" Rachel said.

"The last time we saw him—"

"We?"

"My friends and me." He nodded to indicate the car. Rachel looked past him, saw that there were three other men in the car, that all of them were looking toward the house.

"Oh," Rachel said. "I see."

"Yes," the man said. "We were hunting, and Mike— that's his name, Mike D'Angelo—and Mike, uh, got lost." He grinned, embarrassed. "The last time we saw him he was going into the back of the woods behind your house."

"Did you look there?" Rachel asked.

"Yes, we looked there."

"And you didn't find him?"

"Would I be here if—I'm sorry, no. We didn't find him; we looked, but we didn't find him, Mrs., uh, Mrs."

"I haven't seen him, Mr. Russel. I've been inside all day."

"You're sure?"

"That I've been inside all day? Yes, I'm sure. Now, you'll have to excuse me." She began to close the door. The man stepped forward quickly, held the door. "Would you, uh, tell your husband, when he gets back, that there's a hunter missing and we'd appreciate his help. He can call me at—"

"We don't have a phone, Mr. Russel. And besides, your friend should not have been hunting on our land. If something happened to him . . ." She stopped.

"Yes?"

"Nothing. I'll tell Paul what you said. Now, if you'll excuse me. Please."

The man let go of the door, Rachel closed it softly and watched as he moved slowly up the lawn to the car, got in, and drove away.

Paul arrived a half hour later.

"Insulation," he explained, pushing a huge roll of fiber glass through the doorway and into the kitchen. "We can use it on the upstairs floor, there are four more rolls in the car."

"I'll get my coat," Rachel said, "and help you bring it in."

"Good. Thanks."

"You're late, Paul."

"Yeah, I know. I'm sorry. I had some car trouble, then I had to search all over hell and gone for this stuff and then I went to the phone office and waited around there for a couple hours. I didn't get much accomplished, I'm afraid. I wanted to see if they could get the phone in before the end of the month, but they can't. Don't ask me why—something about schedules and contracts."

"We had visitors, Paul."

A pause.

"Visitors?"

"Some hunters. They wanted to know if they could use our land. I told them no. That's what I thought you'd say. Is it what you'd say?"

"Yes. Yes, it is."

"Other than that, the day's been pretty dull." She grinned.

"Dull?"

She got her coat off the coat tree, shrugged into it. "Dull," she repeated. "Dead dull boring monotonous. Until, that is, about three, and I began worrying about you." She paused. "Bastard," she concluded playfully.

"Dull dead boring monotonous, huh. Sorry to hear it."

"I'm not, Paul. It was heaven."

CHAPTER 25

The shotgun felt heavy, alien, obscene in Paul's hand. It had no place here (what had Rachel said?) in heaven.

He inhaled deeply, caught the musty odor of the forest a hundred yards ahead, the smell of earth around him. A lazy snowfall the night before had vanished shortly after sunrise, moistening the earth, warming it.

Winter, Paul realized, would soon be upon him.

He stared at the twin barrels of the shotgun as he walked. What had he hoped to do with the thing? Kill the approaching winter with it? He thought about that. It was probably the silliest idea that had ever come to him, he concluded. Silly and desperate.

What did he have to fear from the winter that the house and the fireplace and his newly installed insulation and the portable electric heater couldn't take care of? Civilized men are only slowed down by winters, not killed by them. If, that is, they're both civilized and careful (which was, after all, the key to survival under any circumstances).

But if that was so, and if he believed it—as he surely did—why was there that awful fluttering in the pit of his stomach, that second's flow of adrenaline whenever the reality of the coming winter struck him? As it had with the smell of the earth—moist and stinging and cool; the smell of November. The smell of the land in transition.

The November sky, as blue as it was today, caused the fluttering and the flow of adrenaline, too. Because it was a tight, frigid blue—the summer sky was fluid and warm.

He gripped the gun tightly in his left hand. The metal was cold, dispassionate. Dead metal. The gun was death incarnate. Death was its only purpose.

So why had he brought it here? Into heaven.

He stepped cautiously across the narrow stream that bordered this side of the forest. He stopped.

He had come here to kill. He knew it at once and hated it and could do nothing about it. He had come here to kill. Before the winter could.

He was on an errand of mercy. One of God's perverse angels dispatched to ensure heaven a peaceful winter sleep.

He was the sandman.

A short distance to his left a pheasant suddenly took flight, a dozen sheets flapping crazily in a brisk wind. Paul froze for a second, the adrenaline coursing through him, giving him strength momentarily, then sapping it. He snapped his head to the left, watched the pheasant settle to earth fifty yards away. He turned his body to face it, raised the shotgun, aimed.

Sandman.

He touched one of the triggers, felt it give a little.

Sandman.

He squeezed harder, saw the pheasant crouch low, trying to camouflage itself; it was a hen, dull brown, and the short grasses surounding it were nearly the same color.

Sandman.

The pheasant shot into the air again.

200

Paul pulled the trigger tight. The hammer clicked. Paul smiled, relieved. The chamber was empty.

He turned, and took the shallow slope in long, slow strides. He found his way to the clearing easily.

Rachel had never tasted rabbit and the thought of it made her queasy; rabbits were almost like cats, so soft and warm and frisky. Some people made pets of rabbits.

But Paul had told her he was going to bring one home, if one happened to "pose" for him, offered itself. And since, as he had also told her, they might not be able to depend on the grocery store in town for their meat when winter was fully upon them, she had agreed, in order to learn, to steel herself to the task, to cook the rabbit—if he got one— or at least that she'd attempt it.

She rolled over on her shoulder, folded the pillow so her neck and head were horizontal. An hour's nap, that was all. And then she'd do some cleaning, take a bath maybe, do a little reading. But just an hour's nap, first. To shake the cobwebs away; to catch up on all the sleep she'd missed in the last couple weeks.

They were both partly to blame for that, she knew. Their need for one another, their hunger, had not just increased, it had doubled, and redoubled, had become all but an obsession. And she knew also that there were times— even when they were locked together, and their ecstasy was an all-consuming thing—that she was at a distance, watching, grimacing, thinking how distasteful, how wasteful of time, how deadening all of it was, that she was put on the earth for more than merely this.

Later, when she reflected on it, she ascribed those feelings to a latent puritanism instilled in her by her mother— her stolid, no-nonsense, head-always-above-water mother.

Rachel closed her eyes.

The sex—yes, that was part of it. But not all of it. The dreams were just as much a part—the other half.

They were not dreams she wanted to remember; and because she always awoke quickly, sometimes in a sweat, after having them, she remembered little. Only a man—someone with jet-black hair and a day's growth of beard, and anguish splashed all over him and—the thing that caused her to wake, to run, retreat—her own strange, warm feelings upon seeing that face, that anguish, as if it—the poor man's anguish—was inexplicably related to her own pleasure.

But she was exhausted now; perhaps, hopefully—oh, God, please!—that would ensure a deep, dreamless sleep. She thought briefly of taking off her jeans and shirt and decided it would make no difference. She was long past having to make herself comfortable in order to sleep.

Were the doors locked? she wondered. And the windows?

Then her consciousness dimmed and she saw in her mind's eye that the house was wonderfully open, as it should be, open to any of the creatures of the land that might want to come into it. And then sleep overtook her.

Paul had been waiting an hour, the shotgun propped up beside him against the tree trunk where he was sitting, when he heard a soft crackling noise in the underbrush behind him. His body tensed, but he did not move. They obviously wanted to take him by surprise. Let them believe they were; it would ease their caution, make them bolder.

Without moving his head, he glanced at the shotgun. He could reach it, stand, turn, and fire in less than two seconds. Quick. Very quick. But quick enough?

How quick had Lumas been?

The soft, crackling noise repeated itself. It was closer,

Paul thought—closer and more to the right. But it was not time yet. He would wait. Let them come to him.

He chanced a slow glance upward, into the trees that surrounded the clearing; he focused on a huge brown nest in the upper branches of an oak at the other side of the clearing.

He heard a soft, padding sound; like a large cat walking across a stiff rug. They were close. Very close.

He let his gaze fall, his head lowered; he stared momentarily at the ground between his feet, saw a small cream-colored bone there. The bone glistened warmly. *Seductively.*

The word bit into him.

"Shit!" he whispered.

He grabbed the gun. He stood. Turned. Aimed. Fired. Two seconds.

And for Paul, an eternity existed in them. Around them. Like a wheel.

His hand on the cold metal was his hand on his mother's dead face; it was, "Good-bye, Mother." And it was his father's tears. And the other death; that small, wrinkled, white thing at his mother's breast. That grotesquerie. It was the black silhouette where his father lay; the night alone when the dark face touched him, reached out to him, rejoiced in him, in his sadness.

The wheel receded. Went back to its point of rest, the place it had existed for twenty-one years—his years in New York, where he had learned what civilization was, and what his part in it should be.

The point of rest. Just below his consciousness where he could not recognize it or call it up at will. Or remember that it had shown itself again; for the fourth time since he had come back to the house.

He became aware of a dull ache in his shoulder, and

realized he had not held the gun properly, that its vicious recoil had driven the stock hard into his shoulder.

He set the gun down, moved forward a few feet, and bent over. He lifted the mangled raccoon by the scruff of its neck. Its hindquarters were nonexistent, its eyes were open, Paul thought he saw fear and pleading in them. Blood and saliva were welling up in its mouth.

Paul heard himself whisper, "I'm sorry."

He flicked the dead raccoon into the underbrush, turned, picked up the shotgun, and started for home.

Paul got down on one knee beside the bed. He reached out, ran his hand gently over Rachel's back, her waist, her buttocks.

She was never more beautiful, more inviting, he thought, than when she was naked and asleep.

She moaned softly.

"Rachel," he whispered.

There was no reply.

He coaxed her left leg toward him. She moaned again.

"Rachel," he repeated.

He put his hand between her thighs, touched her with the tip of a finger.

He pushed her right leg away, probed with all his fingers. She was open, ready.

She moaned again.

He stood, hurriedly took off his pants, straddled her, inserted himself.

"Paul?" he heard.

He pushed himself into her; once, twice.

"Paul, help me, Paul."

Three times.

She turned her right shoulder toward him, exposed her breast; Paul caught a glimpse of red on the sheet.

Six times.

"Paul, please help me."

Nine times.

He saw that the red on the sheet was her blood, that it also rimmed her nipple, that it had clotted around her breast. Saw it, registered it.

"Oh, Paul, please, please—"

His climax was delicious.

CHAPTER 26

It was early evening. Cold. To the west, the forest was a low black swell on the land capped by a diffused orange glow. From the window, Paul watched quietly, saw the glow weaken, and a star—Venus, he supposed—appear.

Rachel, in her wicker chair across the room, asked, "Will you be long, Paul?"

And Paul answered, "As long as it takes."

"I'll be waiting," she said.

He needn't have said anything, Paul realized—she had asked the question a dozen times in the last half hour, and he had answered it in the same way each time; she merely wanted to break the silence—the silence in the house, and in herself. The deadly stillness that had overcome her in the last week.

Paul, please, please help me. She had said those words again and again. She knew, he realized, that only he could help her, that she was beyond helping herself.

He felt her hand on his shoulder. He turned, put his arms around her, felt her arms go limp.

"Hug me back," he said, trying, in vain, to sound play-ful.

"I can't, Paul."

"Yes, you can."

"Paul. What's happening to me, Paul?"

He pushed her away, held her shoulders at arm's length. Her head was lowered. He put his hand beneath her chin, coaxed her head up.

"Happening to you?" he said.

She closed her eyes briefly; when she opened them, he could see that they were moist. "Happening to you?" he repeated. She turned, hesitated, glanced back at him—*Help me, Paul!*—then crossed the room to her chair.

Lock all the doors, Rachel.

I'll be back before you know it, Rachel.

It's got to be done. If we want to keep them out of the house, it's got to be done.

Reassurance. It was so easy. Part of his role, and, when he wanted to, he played it well.

He shifted the burlap sack to his right hand, the kerosene lamp to his left. He glanced around at the house, saw smoke rising steadily from the chimney, saw Rachel looking out the window in his direction. He waved, though she probably couldn't see him in the darkness.

Part of his role.

He caught the smell of raw venison and clutched the burlap sack tightly to shut the smell off.

A cold night. Still and moonless.

Paul's hands began to numb, sooner, he noted, than he thought they would.

He glanced around again. Rachel was still at the window. He hoped, briefly, that she had seen him wave; it would be good for her.

He stopped on the path, set the burlap sack and the kerosene lamp down. He put his hand in his pocket, pulled out a box of kitchen matches. He'd light the lamp; it would offer a little warmth at least, and some much needed light, which was why Rachel had insisted he bring it.

He lit one of the matches, stooped over, touched the match to the wick, put the globe back, stood with the lantern in hand. He held it out at arm's length. It illuminated a small area of the path in front of him, cast the stones and ruts there in harsh relief. It was good enough, he decided. It would have to be.

He picked up the burlap sack. He walked, slowly at first, then, as his eyes adjusted to the darkness, faster, until he was nearly running.

Paul's silhouette cast by the small glow of the lantern comforted Rachel. It was symbolic; his silhouette and the lantern he carried somehow signified his control, his mastery of the darkness. And also his humanity. And, oddly, his vulnerability. Made him whole. Alive.

Rachel watched the glow recede; he was moving away from her, she realized. She turned from the window, unsettled by the thought that occurred to her.

She crossed the room, pulled her wicker chair over to the desk, sat down. She folded her hands in her lap.

Heaven? she wondered. Heaven?

She opened the middle drawer of the desk, took out a sheet of paper and a pen.

Heaven?

Paul, come home and take me back. Take me back to what I know. The words came to her quickly. She grinned. Take her away from heaven?

"Dear Mother," she wrote, and paused.

She looked quizzically around the room.

Heaven? She turned back to the desk.

"Dear Mother," she read aloud.

"This," she wrote, "will probably be the last letter you will receive from me."

She sat back. She laughed. She glanced around the room again, assuredly now.

Heaven!

She slowly, carefully, thoroughly, crossed out what she'd written.

Paul didn't know why the tears had started. He sat on his heels, lantern on the ground before him, hands over his face, his breathing one great sob and another. The images that came to him held the reason, he knew; but, sobbing, he only watched:

The image of himself as he was at this moment—the image of a man broken;

The image of Rachel, sweet, sensitive, vulnerable, delicious Rachel—the makeshift wooden dagger in hand; the pleading incredulity on her face as he explained that they were going back to the house, that, without telling her in so many words, finding the little girl's body had changed everything, he didn't know how, but it had; Rachel, the vessel, the thing to take pleasure in;

The image of himself telling his new wife about the life they were going to live at the farmhouse, and his relief as her skepticism diminished;

The boy—beauty, perfection reduced by them both to a loathsome, hideous thing, a thing that even death had not rid them of entirely;

Lumas, his old blue eyes set and deadly serious; "The land, Paul. The land . . . creates";

Rachel going on and on about giving the boy a name —she was happy then, loved each moment as if it were a gift, something precious;

Rachel sitting so quietly in her wicker chair, and in

her eyes a constant plea—*Help me, Paul; what's happening to me, Paul? What's happening to us?*

And the children, mere ghosts on the land. Ghosts that had shared his wife with him.

A sharing he had known about for weeks.

A sharing he allowed.

"God help me," he sobbed through his hands.

A sharing he enjoyed.

"Oh, my God, Jesus! What *am* I?"

"What am I?" he heard.

His sobbing abated. He let his hands fall. He opened his eyes.

They were just beyond the circle of lamplight. He could see the fronts of their feet, the suggestion of hands.

"Wh . . . why?" he stammered.

"Why?" he heard.

Three pairs of feet.

"What have we *done* to you?" He waited. They were quiet. "What," he screamed, "have we done to you? For Christ's sake—" He lowered his head, the sobbing began again.

He felt a fluttering at his ear, heard something rustling, like cloth, to his right.

He looked. The burlap sack was gone. He raised his head. He blinked, once, twice, as if resetting his vision, somehow. He saw the rough circle of lamplight; it fluctuated wildly in a sudden breeze. And beyond the light, where the children had been, only darkness.

"They'll eat, Rachel. We'll keep them fed. It's what they want from us; it's *all* they want from us."

"You . . . you saw them, Paul?"

"Yes. I saw something, anyway. It was them, I suppose. It was them."

"And the winter?"

"The winter?"

"The winter will . . . kill them, Paul?"

"Yes, the winter will kill them. God help me, but the winter will kill them. It always has."

"Always has, Paul?"

"Did I say that, Rae? I don't know why I said it. Maybe I'm just . . . grasping, hoping. I don't know why I said it."

"And in the meantime, Paul? While we're waiting."

"Waiting?"

"For the winter. For the winter to kill them."

"We'll keep them fed, as I told you. We'll keep them from going hungry."

"And we'll keep them out of the house?"

"We'll keep them out of the house, Rachel."

"For whose sake, Paul?"

"For your sake. It's all for you."

"Yes, I know it is. I know it is, Paul. It's always been for me, hasn't it?"

"Everything is for you, Rachel. Just remember, please, just remember . . ."

"What? Remember what?"

"That I love you, Rae. That I love you."

"I'm going to bed, Paul. Are you coming with me?"

"Yes. Yes, I'm coming with you."

CHAPTER 27

Rachel put another log on the fire, adjusted it with the poker.

"Can I go with you tonight, Paul?" she called.

Paul, in the kitchen slipping his boots on, called back, "No, I'd rather you didn't. I don't think you're up to it."

Rachel stood, joined her husband in the kitchen. "I'm feeling better," she told him. "Much better. I have to get out of the house."

Paul looked up at her; it was such a simple request— *I have to get out of the house.* So simple.

"No," he said, buckling his second boot. "I'm afraid you can't. Don't ask me why, please. But you can't."

Rachel sighed. "Tomorrow night, then? Can I go tomorrow night? Or don't you believe me?"

"Believe you?" He straightened.

"That I'm feeling better."

"I believe you," he said, and he ached to tell her why she was feeling better, that the cold nights and the cold days had numbed the children, had delivered to them an awful singleness of purpose—to eat, to be fed, to huddle together for warmth.

"I still have the dreams," Rachel said. "But not every night, anymore. Only a couple times a week. And they're not as bad as they were, really they aren't. Say you'll let me go with you tomorrow night. Please."

"Maybe, Rae. I hope so." He picked up the kerosene lamp from the counter, a large plastic bag filled with beef and venison up from the floor. "You sure this will hold, Rachel? This plastic is pretty thin."

"I double-bagged it," she told him.

"Good thinking," he said. *Grasp the mundane, hold tight to it. It's what life is Made of what sanity is made of.*

He went to the back door, Rachel followed, opened it for him. "Thanks," he said. He stepped onto the small square porch, held the lantern out to illuminate the steep flight of steps. "Lock this door," he said, nodding. "And the front door. And all the windows. I'll be back." He took the first step, turned his head to look pleadingly at her; "Whatever you do, Rachel, don't go outside."

"Yes," she said. "Be careful." And she closed the door behind him.

She went into the living room, to the back window. She pushed the curtain aside and watched as he crossed the backyard, made his way to the path north of the house, and started down it. He stopped. Waved. She waved back, then let the curtain fall.

"Paul," she whispered. *It's something I have to do, Paul.* She went to the fireplace, made sure the grate was closed properly, went into the kitchen.

Something I have to do, Paul.

She got her brown wool coat off the clothes tree, put it on, switched the kitchen light off.

She opened the back door, stepped out onto the porch, paused until her eyes adjusted to the darkness.

She took the steps cautiously. At the bottom of the steps, she turned north.

Paul set the lantern down behind him and stared into the dark mass of the forest just ahead. He was waiting. Each night since that first night it had been the same. He would come here, to the end of the path, and, almost immediately, he would hear them coming. They moved very quietly, very quickly, their approach betrayed only by an occasional wisp of laughter—laughter slowed, made fluid, so it sounded almost like song, by the cold, and by their hunger.

Paul listened. He heard, from deep within the forest, the faintly rasping hoot of an owl.

He set the plastic bag down. He cupped his hands to his mouth. "Hello," he called. And he felt suddenly foolish for it, suddenly out of place.

He let his hands fall. He continued to wait.

After a time, he became aware that light snowfall had begun. He watched the small widely scattered flakes drift into the circle of lamplight. He watched, dispassionately at first, as if the snow was telling him some necessary but often-repeated story. He listened. He felt certain he could hear individual flakes settling onto the globe of the lamp and sizzling there, being killed by its warmth.

He saw that among the small nondescript flakes, larger flakes had started to fall.

He gasped, adrenaline pushing through him.

He turned. He ran.

Halfway home he stopped.

"No," he whispered. "No," he screamed. He fell to his knees. He gathered Rachel into his arms.

"Paul," she moaned, "I'm sorry. I'm sorry. I wanted . . ."

"I told you, Rachel. I told you—"

214

"I'm cold, Paul. My clothes. Where are my clothes?"

Paul glanced about, cursed himself for having left the lamp behind, saw, dimly, her coat at the other side of the path. He coaxed her to her feet; she stood unsteadily for a moment, then crumbled. He caught her, set her down gently. "I'll get your coat, Rae. You'll be all right, don't worry. You'll be all right." He got her coat, coaxed her to her feet again, draped the coat over her, took her into his arms, and started for the house, the words "I'm sorry" tripping off his tongue all the way.

MORNING

The snowfall had lasted the night and now the only color on the land was the green of the pines, the brown and gray of the trunks and branches of deciduous trees.

Rachel moved away from the window, got back into bed, pulled the quilt up to her neck. Paul's words of a half hour earlier were still fresh in her mind:

"You'll have nothing more to fear from them after today, I promise you that, Rachel. And when I get back . . . when I get back, we'll make plans."

"Plans?"

"To leave. We should never have come back, I know that now. We should never even have come here, I know that too. This is not our land; it never was. It belongs to them."

"I'm tired, Paul. I just want to sleep."

She closed her eyes.

Sandman, Paul thought. *Sandman.*

He studied the barrel of the rifle; he had left Lumas' shotgun at home. Its range was too limited and it was too messy (he remembered the raccoon; bile crept into his throat). The rifle was more of a long-distance weapon; and it would make a nice, neat hole.

Sandman. Paul grinned. He was a civilized man, it was his duty to enjoy what he had set out to do—avenge, make right, put behind him what had been done to his wife, the perversity he had sanctioned.

Someday, he vowed, he would tell her. Everything. He had to, for his own peace of mind. Even pledging now that, in time, he would tell her would make his life—his knowledge of what had been done, what *he* had done—more bearable.

He heard the babblings of a flight of geese to the south. He looked. It was a large flock, consisting of close to a hundred birds. Because of the distance, they were mere black specks against a backdrop of low gray clouds. Paul raised the rifle, aimed, squeezed the trigger. The hammer clicked. He lowered the rifle, pleased, a feeling of power coming over him.

He reached into his pocket, pulled a cartridge out, loaded the rifle. He was ready now.

He walked quickly, slowed only a little by the snow and the cold air crawling over him.

"Sandman." He was bringing sleep to the troubled, peace to the frenzied. If they could, they would thank him.

He stepped across the stream, noted its edges had iced over, ascended the gentle slope, turned left, and passed beneath the archway and into the forest.

He paused. It had been a long time, weeks since he had been here. And years, decades, since he had seen it this way—the winter resting heavily, quietly, on it.

He moved farther into the forest, head moving, eyes scanning, ears alert all the while. The only sounds that came to him were the sounds his boots made on the new snow; his eyes showed him only the monotony of a gray sky crisscrossed by the bare branches of oaks and honey locusts, and sliced by evergreens.

An inexplicable sadness overcame him as he walked. The sadness of loss, of hope gone; it was, he knew, the sadness of winter and the knowledge of his part in it.

He stopped at the edge of the clearing, saw that a few of the larger bones were jutting above the snow—cream on white; death on sleep.

He wept hard and long.

And realized, as he wept, what his sadness was telling him.

That the winter had done its work. That the children were sleeping at last.

The euphemism annoyed him; he sought to correct it mentally. He found that he couldn't. Found that the proper word would not come to him.

He turned and started for home.

At the archway he paused, turned, and threw the rifle hard, into the forest. Before seeing where the rifle had fallen, he turned again, toward home.

"Rachel, are you asleep?"

"I'm awake."

"They're . . . gone, Rachel."

"Gone?"

"Yes?"

"For good, Paul?"

"For now, Rachel. Until spring. I don't know. Until spring."

"And us?"

"Us?"

"You said we would talk. You said we would make plans."

"We're going to leave, yes. Not right away, not to-morrow. In a week or so. We have to be sure, you see. *I* have to be sure."

"You're not sure?"

"Yes, yes, I am."

"Then why not tomorrow? Why not right now?"

"I'm sorry, I just have to be sure."

"You said you were sure, Paul."

"I am."

"Okay, then. I trust you, Paul."

"And I love you, Rachel. Always remember that."

"I will, Paul. I'd like to sleep now. I've been waiting for you; you're back now. I'd like to sleep."

CHAPTER 28

LEAVING: DECEMBER *1*—EVENING

Rachel closed the book she had been reading, using her forefinger to mark her place. She looked up at Paul; "Did you say anything, Paul?"

He was standing at the back window, had pulled the curtain aside. "No," he said tentatively. Rachel waited. After a moment he continued, "Could you turn that light off for a moment, Rachel?" He glanced around and nodded at the lamp on her writing desk.

"Turn it off?" she said.

"Just for a moment."

She reached over the desk and did as he'd asked.

"Thanks," he said.

He gazed quietly out the window for a long moment.

"What'd you see, Paul?"

He harumphed.

"Paul?"

"You can turn the light on now."

"Did you see something, Paul?" She set her book on the floor, prepared to stand.

He waved at her to stay seated. "It's okay. No. I didn't see anything. Just the lamp reflected in the window."

She switched the lamp on, picked her book up. "How long are you going to stand there like that, Paul? You're awfully jumpy."

"Jumpy?"

"Nervous. And there's no reason for it."

He closed the curtain, went over to the fireplace. "Sorry," he said. He stooped over, spread the grating. "It's getting cold in here; what do you think—should we put some more wood on the fire?" And without waiting for an answer, he went to the left of the fireplace, got two logs from a small pile of logs there, and shoved them into the fireplace. He watched as the logs caught and started to burn. He smiled. "Yes," he said, "that's better."

He went back to the window.

Rachel said, "Would you like me to bring the heater in here?" He caught the sarcasm in her voice.

He sighed. "I was cold, that's all."

"You must have been."

"Don't you think it's cold in here?"

"Not anymore."

"Well, then—"

"Okay, Paul. Okay. Forget it. I guess I just didn't realize. I'm sorry."

"Realize? Realize what?" He turned his head, looked confusedly at her.

"I guess I didn't realize how sensitive you were to the cold, that's all."

He turned back to the window. "Well, now you know."

"Now I know." She returned to her book.

Rachel held the screen door open as Paul stumbled past her, a heavy load of firewood in his arms. "Jesus," he complained, "it's going to be quite a night." He nodded at the firewood. "Take a few of these, Rae."

She let the screen door close, took several logs off the top of the load, and followed him into the living room. They set the logs down next to the fireplace.

"Do you think it's going to snow, Paul?"

He settled into his winged-back chair. "No. The sky's clear. Lots of stars. It's just going to be goddamned cold."

She pointed at the base of the north wall. Paul looked. "Well," she said, "I got the heater going. It should help."

"Yeah," Paul said. "Thanks."

The cat, Mr. Higgins, came in from the kitchen, padded over to Paul, and leaped into his lap.

"Oh, Jesus," Paul muttered, watching, annoyed, as the cat circled a few times, trying for the most comfortable spot. "I don't know why this cat finds me so fucking attractive, Rachel."

Rachel, grimacing a little, lifted the cat gently off his lap, held it, stroked it. "I guess he just knows your true nature, Paul."

"Uh-huh. Well, I wish you'd keep it outside."

"He doesn't like the cold any more than you do, Paul."

Paul stood abruptly, shoved his hands into his pockets, glanced quickly to his right, at the fireplace, to his left, at the heater.

"*What* is the matter, Paul?"

He began to pace the width of the room. "I don't know," he said. "Too much coffee, I guess. I don't know." He stopped in the middle of the room, turned suddenly, went into the kitchen. Rachel stayed in the living room, cat still in her arms. She waited. In a moment, she knew, Paul would come back into the living room, pace some more, then, as if exhausted, plop into his chair. That had been his nightly routine for a week now—the pacing, the preoccupation with staying warm, the hour or so at the back window. That hour would start anytime now, after he had rested for a few minutes. He reappeared from the kitchen. He paused a moment in the doorway. "Put him down, would you?" he said, referring to the cat, and immediately went to his chair. He looked up at her. "I asked you to put him down, Rachel."

"I'd rather not, Paul." She carried the cat to her wicker chair, sat down with it in her lap. "When are you going to calm down, Paul?"

He chuckled derisively. "Calm down? You mean like *you've* calmed down?"

"Yes. At least I've made the effort."

"You most certainly have done that, haven't you? My God, have you no conscience at all?"

"That's not fair, Paul. It's cruel. You know what I've been through here."

"Yes, I do. And any sane woman . . . for Christ's sake, any *sane* woman would have, would have . . ."

"Gone over the edge?"

"Yes, precisely."

"Is that what you want, Paul?"

He stood, hesitated.

Rachel repeated, "Is that what you want, Paul?"

"Of course not!" he snapped.

"I try not to think about it, Paul. And when I do think about it, I think about the good, only the good."

He grinned at her. "I'll bet you do."

"What in hell does *that* mean?"

His grin vanished suddenly. "Nothing," he said. "Forget it. Nothing." He went to the back window.

Rachel put the cat down, stood; "Paul, I . . ." She joined him at the window.

"Yes?" he said. He was holding the curtain aside with his left hand. Rachel put her hand on his hand. "Tell me, Paul."

He glanced quizzically at her, then out the window again. "Tell you?" he said, his voice expressionless. "Tell you what?"

"What you've been keeping from me all these weeks. I want to know. I need to know."

"I haven't been keeping anything from you. What happened to you—it was something that happened to both of us. We got . . . carried away. We got carried away."

Magic!

"No, Paul. It's more than that. I know it is. You and I getting carried away doesn't explain a thing, not—"

"Quiet!" he hissed. She felt his hand tighten.

"What is it, Paul?"

"Quiet!" he repeated. "Turn that light out."

"Do you see something, Paul? What—"

"Do as I say, Rachel. Now!"

She crossed the room, turned the lamp off, went back to the window, tried to nudge him aside. "Wait!" he ordered.

"What do you see, Paul?"

He stayed quiet for a moment.

"Paul?"

"I don't know. A light. Something. A light. Venus, maybe." He took a step to his right. "You look."

Rachel looked. The thin covering of snow seemed vaguely luminous, as if the ground beneath were dully phosphorescent; it was a phenomenon Rachel had noted

223

many times, even before coming to the house, and had wondered about: Had the snow always seemed to glow like that?

Above the western horizon, and to the south and north, and extending to where the window cut her view off overhead, the stars were of a hundred different magnitudes: Familiar groupings—the Big Dipper to the northwest, Orion to the south—seemed crowded, seemed made into whole new constellations by lesser stars.

On the western horizon, the forest—featureless and black now—inserted itself between the earth and sky.

Rachel squinted.

At the forest's center, she could see a faint, randomly pulsating, reddish light; as if, she thought, the forest had suddenly become monolothic, a great dark mass, and someone had punched a very small hole in it, and the last rays of the sun were trying to push through.

Rachel found that the light was easier to see if she focused a little to its right or left, just as one keeps a very faint star in view.

She closed her eyes, shook her head. She opened her eyes, studied the light again briefly. "It's a star," she said, "Mars is red, isn't it? It's Mars, Paul."

He coaxed her away from the window. "No," he said. "Mars is over the eastern horizon this time of year."

The light vanished suddenly, as if a curtain had been drawn over it. "It's gone, Rachel."

She went to the desk, switched the lamp on, sat in her chair. "It was nothing, Paul. Just Venus, as you said. Sit down, I'll read to you."

He continued to look out the window. "Read to me?" he said.

"Yes. Maybe it'll calm you down."

"I don't want to be calmed down."

"Well, I want to calm you down. Now, please . . ."

"No. If you want to read to me, that's fine. But I'm not going to move from this window."

"Okay, then." She picked up the book she'd been reading, opened to its first page: "London was having one of her days," she read. "Outside, the streets glistened dully with half frozen sludge and the air was thick, dark and apparently contaminated with poison gas."

DECEMBER 3

"It's there again," Paul said. He gestured for Rachel to join him at the window.

"What's there?" Rachel asked. She looked up at him.

"That light. The one we saw yesterday."

"Oh. That."

"Come take a look, Rachel."

She sighed. "It's just a star, Paul."

"Rachel, please."

"For God's sake—"

"Rachel, do as I say."

"Chauvinist!"

"This is not the time for jokes, Rachel. I need your help here."

"Who's joking, Paul?" She stood. "I hope that when we get back to New York"—she crossed the room—"you'll mellow a bit."

He nodded. "What do you think, Rae."

She looked. "A star," she said, obviously unconcerned. She turned, started for her chair. Paul caught her by the shoulder. "Look again, Rachel."

"You're hurting me, Paul."

He loosened his grip. "Sorry."

She turned back to the window. She glanced at him: *I've been hurt enough here, Paul,* her eyes told him.

225

"I said I was sorry, Rachel."

She looked out the window again, quietly.

"Well?" Paul coaxed.

"It's brighter, isn't it?" she said finally.

"Yes," Paul agreed. "I noticed that."

"If I didn't know better, Paul, I'd say it's some kind of fire, a campfire."

"That's what I thought."

She studied the light for a full minute. Then: "Do you remember those hunters I told you about?"

"Yes."

"Well, maybe it's them."

"But that was a month ago, Rae."

"It could be some other hunters."

"I suppose."

Rachel stepped away from the window. "Well, then," she began, "we're agreed. It's just some hunters." She went back to her chair. "Some stupid dimwit hunters who have nothing better to do with their time than freeze their foolish butts off. And if they do, they deserve it, that's all I can say." She opened her book. "Now, sit down, Paul. I'll read to you some more."

DECEMBER 4—AFTERNOON

Dear Mother,

This will be my last letter before we see you again. We'll be leaving in two days. I'd like to explain everything to you here and now, sort of get it all off my chest. But, to be truthful, I don't believe I'll ever be able to explain it. I don't believe I'll ever be able to *understand* it, let alone explain it.

Are we running? Yes. That's a fair assessment, I'd say. I can't tell you precisely what we're running from;

Paul's word for it is "ghosts," and I don't think I could do any better than that.

The important thing, the necessary thing, for both of us, is that we *are* running. This is going to sound terribly melodramatic, Mother, and you're going to ask me about it when I see you, and I'm going to have to plead ignorance, but, if we don't run now, we won't be able to run later. I'm sure of that. This is a matter of survival.

I want to ask you a favor. When we get back, when you see us again, please don't ask any pointed questions. You'll be burning to ask them, I know, and I'll be burning to answer, but, well, both of us, Paul and I, have a lot of questions to answer between ourselves first, and we've got a lot of time to make up for, a lot of things to put behind us.

For now, let me assure you that we are both well, though a little tired—emotionally—and that unless something unexpected happens we should see you within the week.

Paul sends his love. And so do I.

Rachel

EVENING

"It *is* a fire," Paul said. "And it's closer."

Rachel called from the kitchen, "What did you say, Paul? Your coffee's almost ready."

"I said come here," Paul called back. He waited. Presently, Rachel appeared at his side.

"What is it, Paul?" She handed him a cup of coffee. He took it and stepped away from the window. "Look there," he said. He held the curtain aside. Rachel stepped up to the window.

"Oh," she said. "It's snowing, isn't it?"

227

"That's not what I called you in here for, Rachel."

"Yes," she said. "I know. I can see the fire."

"It's closer, Rae."

"Is it?" She squinted into the darkness. "You're right. It is closer."

Paul went into the kitchen. Rachel followed him with her eyes. "What are you going to do, Paul?"

"I've got to be sure," he called. "I've got to be sure."

She listened as he put on his boots and coat.

"Sure of what, Paul?"

"I'll be back soon, Rae." He paused. "Where's that kerosene lamp?"

"Sure of *what*, Paul?"

"Did you put it in the closet?"

She heard the closet door open. She went into the kitchen.

"Sure of what, Paul?"

"What are you talking about? Where's the lamp?"

"I don't know. Don't we have a flashlight or something?"

"No, just that stupid lamp." He slammed the closet door. "Dammit, I can't go out there without it."

"Why do you want to go out there at all?"

He went to the back door, pulled it open. "Lock this after me," he said, and he was gone.

Paul could not understand the frenzy within him. He had known, he knew; the almost mystical knowledge that had overcome him a week before had told him: Winter had done what winters always did here. It had killed. It had released Rachel and him from a torment, a nightmare from which they had been unable to release themselves.

He found that he was walking with the aid of memory—the memory of a thousand walks down this path; that, in the nearly total darkness, he was automatically avoiding obstacles he had avoided a thousand times in daylight.

He tried to study the thing that had driven him from the house, tried to take it apart. There was anger in it, he knew—a passionate, wordless anger, the anger that comes from frustration. And there was pity, too; pity for himself, and for Rachel. And for the children. For he had no doubt now that it was they who had built the fire, they who sustained it, they who wanted its light to tell him of their presence.

He glanced around, saw Rachel looking out the window at him. He thought briefly of waving, but realized that she couldn't see him.

Their marriage, he felt certain, was at an end. There were too many unanswered questions, too much pain to reflect upon. Now, while they remained at the house, they could cling to one another, depend on one another; they had to. But when the city surrounded them again, it would be time to answer the questions, time to reflect upon the pain. And their love, as strong as it was, would not be able to hold them together. She would always be a stranger to him. He would always be a stranger to her.

His foot connected with something metallic. He stopped, bent over. It was the lamp. He picked it up. He remembered. This was the spot where he had found Rachel the week before, the place she had fallen, had succumbed, had given herself to . . .

"Damn you!" It was a high, piercing scream. Its pitch, from his throat, shocked him. He threw the lantern to the ground. The globe shattered tinnily. The effort displeased him. His scream had displeased him.

"Goddamn you! I'll kill you all! I'll kill you all!"

And he ran. Hard.

He stopped. He could hear the stream just ahead—because it was fast-flowing, it wouldn't freeze over until midwinter.

He smelled wood burning. He looked to his left. The upper branches of the archway were bathed in a flickering orange light.

Goddam you! But the curse went unuttered.

Curses, he realized at once, and anger, were alien to them, something beyond their comprehension.

He moved south, off the path, and into his fields.

He stopped again. He watched quietly. Reverently. He owed them that much. His curses, his anger, had no place here, in their midst; this was their cathedral.

And as he watched, and saw their faces turn occasionally, saw the eyes, expressionless, look in his direction, watched the firelight play on the smooth dark skin, watched hands touch hands and arms and bellies—as if giving warmth and receiving it; as if reexperiencing, as if reveling in what they were—he knew that they were doing him a kindness. That he was privileged, somehow. That few men, if any, had been allowed to see what he was seeing.

Their slow and graceful deaths.

"Did you talk to them, Paul?"

He sat in one of the kitchen chairs. "Talk to them?"

"Yes. Those hunters. Did you ask them what they thought they were doing—building fires on our land, in our woods?"

Paul sighed. "No. No, I didn't talk to them. They're not going to hurt anybody, Rachel. They'll be gone soon."

"You were out there quite a long time, Paul. What did you do if you didn't talk to them?"

"Nothing. I was just . . . I was just being careful. It was pitch-black out there, without the lantern, I mean."

She came over to him, put her hands on his shoulders. "They'll be gone soon? How do you know that, darling?"

Darling. He smiled wistfully, thought of thanking her.

"I just know it," he said. "How long can they stay out there in the cold?"

"Well, I just hope you're right, that's all."

"We'll be leaving soon, anyway, Rachel. So what does it matter?" He turned his head, looked questioningly at her.

She shrugged. "I guess it doesn't matter." She paused. "Here, let me get this coat off you."

"No. Not right now, please. I'm still cold. God, I'm chilled to the bone."

"You're going to start sweating if you keep that coat on, silly." She leaned over him, started unbuttoning the coat. He grabbed her hand, held it tightly. "No, please, Rachel."

She stared incredulously. "Paul . . . Paul, your hand! What's wrong with your hand?"

He looked; an almost inaudible gasp came from him. He instinctively withdrew the hand, clasped it in his other hand, put both hands between his knees. "Nothing," he whispered. "Nothing. They're cold. They're cold. I didn't have any gloves. It's frostbite. It's nothing." He stood quickly. "I've got to get them warm, that's all. I've got to get them warm."

And he ran into the living room.

When Rachel followed, she found him in front of the fireplace, hands extended over the fire. The ugly brown splotches she had seen on them only a minute before had all but vanished.

DECEMBER 5—EVENING

"They're halfway to the house now, Paul." She turned, faced her husband; he was sitting quietly in his chair. "Paul?"

231

"I heard you."

She turned back to the window, saw two fires—one bright, and large, and undulating, the other its dim, off angle miniature—its secondary image on the window glass.

And she saw the three dark figures seated around the fire; she sketched in her mind the geometry, the symmetry those still figures represented.

Her eyes lowered. Her gaze fell on the four remaining snow-covered piles of wood, the beehives, the lopsided pyramids Paul had asked her to build weeks before.

She glanced at him. His eyes were closed now. He seemed in pain, somehow, seemed to be undergoing some deep inner turmoil.

She looked again at the bright, warmly undulating fire.

And awareness, as bright and as sure as the flames, came to her.

"They're not hunters at all, are they?" she said. She waited.

After a long moment, Paul answered, "No, Rachel, they aren't." He opened his eyes, kept his gaze on the opposite wall. "I was going to tell you."

"Were you?"

"Yes. Yes, I was. I was going to tell you. Later. After we left."

"Then we *are* leaving?"

"Yes, we're leaving. We're leaving tomorrow. Early."

She looked out the window again. "I'll understand, Paul . . . If you don't want to leave, I'll understand."

"Why would I want to stay?" He waited for her answer. She said nothing. "I asked why I would want to stay, Rachel."

She took a deep breath, held it a moment. "How soon will they die, Paul? Do you think that fire of theirs keeps them warm?"

Paul looked at her; out of the corner of her eye she saw that he was looking. She turned her head; their eyes met. He smiled a relieved smile. "You know, don't you, Rachel?"

She extended her hand. He took it. "Yes, Paul, I do."

Paul stood, his hand still holding hers.

"Come here," she coaxed. He joined her at the window.

"It's their last night, isn't it, Paul?"

He squeezed her hand; his eyes watered suddenly. "And our first night," he said. She leaned against him. "Rachel, they want us to stay."

"I know it."

"And I wish we could. But . . . I've . . . I've grown beyond them, I think. I've grown beyond them."

Rachel said nothing.

"I thought," Paul continued, "that I owed them something. And perhaps I do. But if I owe them anything, I owe them myself, not you."

Again Rachel was quiet.

"Do you understand what I'm saying, Rachel?" He waited.

"I don't know, Paul." A whisper. "I think I do, but . . . it's something . . . something I'd rather not face right now. Perhaps in time, but not right now." She paused; Paul could feel her tears through his shirt. "Look," she said, her voice quaking, "it's started to snow."

"Yes," Paul said. "Yes," he repeated. "Now the winter will do its work."

LATE EVENING

Even as she struggled out of sleep, Rachel knew the source of the acrid smell that filled her nostrils. She nudged

Paul, asleep beside her. "Paul," she said aloud. "Wake up, Paul."

"It's too cold," he groaned.

She shook him. "Paul, Paul, wake up!"

He opened his eyes. "What's wrong? What's . . . what's that smell?"

He sat up suddenly. "My God, Rachel . . . it's . . ." He swung his feet to the floor, he stood, grabbed the doorknob tightly. He yanked his hand back. He cursed sharply.

Rachel scrambled out of bed.

"The doorknob's hot," Paul explained. "It's the house, it's . . . it's . . ."

"No," Rachel said steadily. "No. It can't be."

And they both saw the band of flickering yellow light beneath the door.

Paul ran to the window, opened its lock, pushed up. The window refused to move.

He glanced around. "Rachel," he ordered, "the washbasin! On the dresser? The washbasin, quick! Give it to me!"

Rachel grabbed the washbasin. "I don't understand, Paul. I don't understand," she said as she crossed the room. "We put the fire out. Why do you want this?" She gave him the washbasin. "I don't understand. Please, Paul . . ." She turned. "I don't understand." She crossed to the door. She put her hand on the doorknob. "Why don't we just—"

"Rachel, no!" Paul shouted.

She let go of the doorknob. She stepped back. Her body shook.

"Don't open that door, Rachel!"

"Yes," she murmured, "Yes. I'm sorry."

Paul brought his arm back, washbasin in hand.

Rachel turned, faced him. "They did this, Paul. They want us to stay."

Paul brought his arm forward. "No," he whispered.

He stopped its movement halfway to the window. "No!" he screamed. "No, you won't, you can't, I won't let you, she's not yours!"

He crossed the room.

He threw the door open.

And in the second before the fire swept over her, Rachel saw the three dark, perfect faces beyond the window.

And she understood.

A smile started on her lips.

The words "Thank you, Paul" came to her.

THE MORNING

The child, a boy, is intrigued by the gleaming, bulbous thing in the ashes. He reaches for it. A girl nearby reaches at the same time. "I don't understand," she says, "I don't understand." The boy, screeching, lashes out at her. She moves off, grunting.

The boy picks up the bulbous thing, and turns it around and around, studying it. He puts it into his mouth, tests it with his tongue, bites it, throws it to the ground, and continues searching.

One of the girls lifts a soot-blackened jar from the ashes. She studies it hopefully. Finally, she tosses it to one side; it shatters against the dark bulk of the stove. Soon, a pungent odor wafts over to her, and she turns quickly and moves over to the remains of the jar. Then the other children are upon her, variously tearing at her, trying to push her away, and tearing at the stuff from within the jar. Soon there is no trace of it. And the children continue searching.

No longer are their bellies constantly full. Or their skins warm. No longer have they time for desire.

And so they poke through the ashes.

And tear fitfully at the one to find the bones.

235

While, around them, the frigid morning collects itself.
A December morning. Quiet. But with promise.
In time, there will be no more bones.
And winter is upon them.